Red on the Right

SARAH WELK BAYNUM

Red on the Right

Editor: Laurie Berglie

Cover Designer: GermanCreative on Fiverr

ISBN:

979-8-9863339-2-2

Website:

https://sarahwelkbaynumauthor.com/

Contents

Chapter One

Emma Walker closed her eyes while listening to the ocean's waves crashing against the sandy beach.

The sound of the tide was loud enough to drown out almost everything else. Everything, that is, except her racing mind. She sighed audibly, frustrated that even her happy place, the ocean, wasn't able to take her mind off her thoughts today.

Emma's eyes flew back open as they locked in on the waves a few feet from where she lay on a beach towel. She sat halfway up, putting her elbows under her as she watched seagulls scurrying away from another incoming wave.

Down the beach, she could hear laughter. She decided not to look this time. Yesterday, it had been a couple that looked blissfully happy; it was nauseating. At least, it was nauseating now. Not so long ago that had been her and Liam.

"Liam," she thought, feeling the nausea heighten when his name ran across her thoughts.

Emma sat all the way up now, knowing the beach nap she had been trying to take for half an hour was not happening. Mandy lay on the beach towel next to her and had been asleep for some time now.

"Must be nice," Emma murmured softly to herself.

"What must be nice?" Mandy asked, rolling over on her back, turning in Emma's direction as she squinted against the bright, mid-day sun.

"Nothing. Sorry Mandy, I didn't mean to wake you up," Emma replied, feeling bad for waking her friend.

"It's ok, I was already half-awake anyway because I kept getting hot," Mandy said, sitting up too.

"Want to get in the water then?" Emma suggested.

"Definitely," Mandy said, as she dusted sand off her legs.

The two young women headed towards the ocean. They walked into the water until they were waist deep, and Emma enjoyed the cool water against her skin.

Mandy tossed her a look; clearly, she was still wondering what Emma had been mumbling about a minute ago. The thing about long term friendships is sometimes you don't need words; one look and she knew Mandy wasn't letting it go.

"Just another nauseatingly happy couple," Emma replied to Mandy's unspoken question.

"You do know you have two very attractive guys who are both crazy about you, right?" Mandy asked, putting her hands on her hips as she gave Emma a teasing smile. Emma knew Mandy was trying to lighten the mood with her typical humor.

"That's exactly the problem," Emma said, shaking her head and turning towards the horizon.

It had been exactly one week today that Liam had dropped the proposal bomb on her when she had least expected it. Truly, it had been a shock.

Emma had run out of the house and away from Liam without a reason or an answer. When she had finally stopped to slump against a tree, she had hoped to find some clarity as she sat alone for almost an hour.

Luckily for her, Emma ran the opposite direction from the way Liam needed to take to get back to the highway. She simply couldn't face him, or Michael for that matter, until she had time to process what had happened. After all, besides her career, marriage was the most important decision someone could make. And the moment Liam asked her to marry him, Emma realized that she had absolutely no idea what to say. Which is why she ran and didn't stop running.

Emma had later asked Mandy what went on after she made her great escape.

After an hour had passed, Mandy went looking for her, knowing something about the conversation had gone terribly wrong. Thank God for Mandy and her best friend intuition. Mandy had apparently handled Liam so that there would not be yet another physical altercation at the Live Oaks Farm.

Liam had returned to the front of the house when Emma didn't come back and asked if Mandy knew where Emma had gone.

"Liam, I think it's best you go home. I'll check on Emma and be sure she contacts you when she is ready," Mandy had told Liam that night. Luckily, Michael was at the barn when Liam had finally emerged from the house.

Emma remembered hearing his sports car tear down the back road, watching his taillights fade into the distance knowing that, once more, she had broken his heart.

Shortly after, Emma remembered hearing Mandy calling her name. It wasn't long before Mandy found her slumped against that tree, eyes red and puffy.

"Liam proposed to me, and I don't know what to do," Emma had managed to choke out. Her heart felt torn in half between the feelings she now had for Michael and the history she had with Liam.

Mandy had sat with her for another fifteen minutes, letting her ramble on about nothing as her mind processed what her heart couldn't.

"I can't go back home right now," Emma had said after the emotions had let up a little.

"Why don't we take a trip then? You can get some distance, clear your head, and make a logical decision. I still have plenty of time off per my boss, no thanks to being kidnapped, and I could use a little vacation myself anyway," Mandy had suggested.

It was genius really. What better way to get some perspective than away from the real world?

"Can we go to the beach?" Emma asked, knowing the ocean was the only place that could possibly help her get her mind right.

"That's a perfect idea!" Mandy had replied excitedly. It had been a very long time since the two friends had taken a girls trip anyway. There couldn't be a better time to do so than right now.

"I'll text Liam, tell him I'm going on a trip with you, and that I need some time to think. But what about Michael?" Emma asked, her bottom lip quivering at the thought of hurting him too.

"Let me talk to Michael. If you don't want to tell him about the proposal, we don't have to. We can just say we wanted to take a girls trip and hope he doesn't press for details," Mandy replied, shooting Emma a sympathetic look.

"It would only break his heart," Emma replied shaking her head. "Don't tell him about the proposal, just say after everything we both went through recently that we need some girl time."

After that, Emma headed straight back to the house and packed a bag. Mandy headed to the barn to tell Michael what they discussed. From what Mandy told her, Michael seemed a little confused but told Mandy to have a good time and that he and Sam would have things at the barn covered.

Mandy said she wasn't entirely sure if he bought it and that perhaps he was a little suspicious of such an impromptu trip. Not to mention that Emma had sent Mandy to tell him instead of Emma telling him herself. That alone was strange, and Michael knew it.

Emma and Mandy were on the road to the beach thirty minutes later. Mandy drove and Emma booked a hotel on the road. They had decided to drive south and to visit the gulf coast. Emma remembered her dad saying that his parents used to take trips to Treasure Island all the time when he was growing up. It had been on her bucket list for some time, and with it being about two hours away, it seemed like the perfect time to visit.

With so many memories of Liam and even some with Michael on the Atlantic Ocean side of Florida, the change of pace seemed ideal.

Emma had never been to the gulf coast, and it did not disappoint. The calm, crystal-clear blue-green water was breathtaking. And for a little while, with her best friend at her side, Emma forgot all about the drama back home.

That is, until today. At first, the beach and all the activities they had been doing was enough to occupy her mind. But after a week here, it was as if her mind had caught up with her and even the ocean couldn't calm her racing mind.

Emma was surprised at how little Mandy had pressed her to discuss the situation. On two occasions Mandy had casually asked her if she was ready to talk, but both times Emma had said she wasn't ready. Mandy, despite normally being the type of friend that would typically press for details anyway, had backed off. Perhaps even she understood the gravity of the decision Emma was being forced to make. A decision she had not expected to have to make any time soon. After all, she and Liam were broken up. Or so she thought.

Staring out at the water, Emma couldn't help but recall their relationship before the distance between them had taken its toll. She had been happy, hadn't she? Before things became strained that is. It seemed like another lifetime ago that Emma met Liam at college back in Ohio. It felt almost fated when they ran into each other in Wellington. His good looks and charm had reeled her back in like no time had passed between meeting back home and re-connecting in Florida.

Emma watched the sun gleam off the water in front of them as she continued to let her mind churn over her options.

It had been like a fairytale. That is, until she had been stalked, which seemed to bring them together quickly given the life-or-death situation. But it had also robbed them of what the beginning stages of a relationship should look like. It wasn't long after that she was back in Ocala. Had she really given Liam a real shot? Or had she given up too quickly when things got hard?

Not that she entirely regretted breaking things off; at the time, it was the right choice. Liam was hyper-focused on his career and so was she. They lived too far away to have a real relationship. So now that he was promising her what she needed months ago, *did* that change everything?

The glaring issue here was that it was no longer just about whether or not she and Liam could work through things with this new promise of commitment and less distance between them all the time.

Now, there was someone else that complicated things even more.

Michael.

Emma closed her eyes, her hands gently touching the surface of the water as she thought about how things had changed so much between her and Michael in just a few weeks. She still remembered the electricity between them when they had kissed that night in the rain. It had been her move.

Emma tried to put herself back in that moment. What had she been thinking? Mostly, she hadn't. But there has always been something else lingering in the background of her friendship with Michael.

He had confessed his feelings to her while they searched the Ocala Forest for Mandy, confirming her suspicions that he had felt more than friendship for some time. Emma remembered the feeling of everything falling into place between them after that. Michael had risked his life several times for her now. Certainly, that was something she should take into account.

If she did decide to marry Liam, she had a pretty strong feeling that Michael would no longer be welcome in her world. That, of course, was complicated considering he worked with her at Live Oaks Farm. Still, Emma saw no way around being with Liam and staying friends, or even co-workers, with Michael. Too much had happened between them, let alone the altercation between Liam and Michael when Liam had first discovered Michael kissed her.

Was she ready to push Michael completely out of her life to be with Liam? At the end of the day, that seemed to be what it came down to.

Emma opened her eyes and caught Mandy staring at her.

"You ok?" Mandy asked softly, reading Emma's distressed facial expression.

"Just thinking about...well, everything," Emma replied quietly.

"You know I'm here if you need me," Mandy said, more as a statement.

"I think pretty soon I'll be ready to talk about it," Emma admitted.

And she was. She knew this little vacation was quickly coming to a close. Back home, reality would hit hard and when it did, she needed to be sure of what she wanted.

It had been strange not talking to Michael all week long. Or Liam for that matter, considering they had not been apart long, and he had asked her to marry him only a week ago.

Emma shook her head, clearing her mind. This was a near impossible decision. In the end, someone was going to be heartbroken. She just didn't know who that was yet.

elle

Mandy thanked the waitress when she brought back her credit card and receipt. Emma set her fork down on her now empty plate.

"Nobody does seafood like the Florida coast," Mandy said, eating the last bite of food on her own plate which was now all but scraped clean.

"That's for sure. Gosh, I'm going to miss dinner views like this," Emma said, as her eyes passed over the setting sun and the beachside view from their table.

"We should take a sunset beach walk since it's our last night here," Mandy suggested, her eyes looking out on the beach in front of them as well.

"That's a great idea!" Emma said, taking one last sip of her almost polished off pina colada.

The two women stood up and headed out of the restaurant's patio area, stepping onto the sandy beach. The sand was cooler now, and both of them pulled off their sandals to walk barefoot down the coast.

Emma had always heard the sunsets on the gulf coast were beyond stunning, and they were right. An array of colors filled the sky behind the crystal blue water.

They walked along in silence on the part of the sand were the foamy waves intermittently washed over their feet as they strolled along.

"Mandy...what should I do?" Emma asked, suddenly breaking the silence. Mandy's head whipped around to look at her, eyes wide in surprise that Emma had finally opened up about the situation.

"Oh, Em. I wish it was that simple. If I could give you the right answer you know I would! But you're the only one who can answer that question," Mandy said, her eyes reflecting her sympathy for what her friend was going through.

"I know," Emma replied with a sigh.

They walked a little while longer in silence, Emma's mind churning over every-thing she had considered earlier that day. "Want to sit and watch the sun finish setting?" Emma asked.

"Sure," Mandy replied. Mandy had been taking peeks at the breathtaking sky as they walked along too.

Emma sat on the powder soft white sand with Mandy beside her. Mandy had a thoughtful look on her face as she turned toward Emma again and wrapped her arm around her friend's shoulders.

"Em, my mom gave me some advice once. I remember it was after my heart was broken; I was maybe eighteen years old, and it was my first love who had broken up with me. Back then, you think every guy you date could be *the one*," Mandy said with a laugh. "But I remember I asked her how do you know the person is really *the* one? I was thinking just now and her words came to my mind, and I hope they help you the way they helped me back then. She told me you should choose a man who feels like your dearest friend. Mom always said after the honeymoon stage ends, what you're left with is friendship. And most importantly, is he the person you can't live without? So maybe just consider that; who is the man you can't see your life without?"

Emma looked back at her friend, meeting her gaze. Was it really that simple? It made sense. And truly, there was no way both Liam and Michael could be a part of her life going forward anyway. At the end of the day when she chose, she would be essentially choosing one and exiling the other.

So really, all she needed to do was figure out which of them she couldn't see herself living life without.

"Mandy, that might be the best advice you have ever given me," Emma replied.

"Good, I'm glad it helped," Mandy said, squeezing Emma's hand before she returned her gaze back to the now almost set sun.

Emma looked out at the horizon too, taking a deep breath of salty air.

"Who can I not live without?" she thought.

They watched as the sun disappeared behind the ocean and then sat there until it was completely dark. But by then, Emma had a pretty good idea of who it was that she didn't want to live without.

Have you ever had a dream that seemed so real that you weren't sure what to believe? What if it was true? And if it wasn't, would you want to retreat back to that dream in hopes to live in that reality a little longer? Sometimes life is stranger than a dream, and the only way to wake up is to face what lies hidden in your soul.

For Emma, last night's dream was exactly that. It was as if her soul was trying to tell her something. She just hoped that *something* was the right choice.

Emma heard Mandy zipping up her suitcase as she opened her eyes and looked around the hotel room a moment as she got her bearings. She still was trying to figure out where her dream ended and where reality began.

"Good morning, friend," Mandy said.

"Good morning," Emma said groggily, sitting up.

"We better get on the road soon, our check-out time is in half an hour," Mandy said, looking at the clock on the nightstand.

"I'll pack up," Emma replied, still feeling half asleep.

Her dream still lingered in the back of her mind. She hoped it was a sign she was making the right decision.

"Did you still want to stop in a few of those beach towns on the way back home like we discussed? I wasn't sure if you were eager to get back home...," Mandy began.

"No way, let's make those stops. As much as I miss the horses, I am not in any hurry to break a heart," Emma said, still feeling anxious about her decision.

Still though, it wouldn't make the fall out of that decision any easier.

The two young women packed up Mandy's car and checked out. They planned to take the road that ran parallel to the ocean for as long as they could before needing to cut inland towards Ocala.

They drove north, stopping at the most adorable town with a boardwalk that looked like it came right out of a travel agent's brochure.

Emma checked her phone for the first time in a while as they waited for the dessert they had just ordered, despite the fact both of them were all but overflowing from the lunch they just had.

"Mandy! I just got a text from Cathy. They just officially sent Clint to jail for charges of kidnapping and the ransom money they took from Cathy. It looks like he will be in prison awhile," Emma said.

"What about the thirty thousand dollars he stole from her?" Mandy replied, wide-eyed.

"They are working on getting that back to her this week, thank God," Emma said. Cathy had been so generous to wire that kind of money on a moment's notice the minute she knew her best friend's life was in danger.

The two women sat in silence processing the events of those days until the waitress interrupted them with their orders of chocolate cake.

Endless miles of ocean on their left and far too much food had proved to be the perfect recipe for getting Emma's mind off of what tomorrow would bring.

Emma ran through that tough conversation she would soon be having with someone she cared so deeply about as she stared out the car window. He would be crushed and the complications of what that meant for her future work situation were still swirling around in her mind.

"You're making the right choice," she thought, reminding herself of the countless hours she had spent considering her options.

Emma watched the miles of Florida's coast roll by, and she let herself think about the upside of that dreaded conversation. When it was over, she could finally move on with the person she knew without a doubt she couldn't live without.

That was worth it all, at the end of the day.

Chapter Two

It had been late when Emma and Mandy had pulled into Live Oaks Farm last night. So late that Emma decided not to say hi to Valentine at the expense of waking up the rest of the barn. Besides, she needed a good night's sleep before the tough conversation this day was about to bring her.

Emma picked up her phone and called a number as her stomach did back flips. This was really it. The end of an era, in a way.

"Hello?" a male voice answered, sounding surprised by her call.

"Hey, it's me. Sorry, I know this is out of the blue and we haven't spoken, and I'm sure you're confused about why I disappeared to the coast for a week. I'm also sorry I didn't give you a heads up, but I'm standing outside. Can you come out so we can talk?" Emma asked, her voice low and soft.

Emma was sure her own heart was about to be breaking right alongside his. After all, she still cared about him deeply. But a decision had to be made and she couldn't drag it out any longer than she already had.

So this morning when Emma woke up, she beelined directly to his place to tell him the news. It was only fair to not string him along any more than she already had. And Emma was sure she couldn't take another minute of the pressure this decision had put on her.

Liam stepped out of his aunt's estate with an expression that still gave away his surprise at her sudden return. Not to mention driving over three hours to Wellington out of the blue.

Emma had not spoken to Liam or Michael since the day they had left for Treasure Island, so she couldn't blame him for wondering why she had suddenly appeared at his doorstep.

His eyes locked onto hers, searching them for the meaning of this visit. He surely wanted to know one thing: was she here to accept his proposal or break up with him, for good this time.

Emma took three steps toward him, closing the gap between them. She threw her arms around his neck and pulled him into a hug. She breathed in the smell of the cologne that lingered on his collared shirt. He looked like he had just finished getting dressed for the day. That made sense she supposed, considering it was just after 7:00 am. When she woke up that morning, there was only one thing on her mind: talking to Liam.

"Emma," Liam said softly, pulling back and looking her in the eye as he put both hands on either side of her face. "Why are you here," he asked, his eyes begging for answers.

Emma bit her lip, trying to remind herself of why she was here.

"Liam, you are a great guy...," Emma cut herself off, realizing the similarity of her words to those of her ex-boyfriend, Jordan's, when he had ended things. Ugh, she hated this.

Emma shook her head, looking away from his gaze a moment as she collected her thoughts.

"Let me start over. Liam, this has been an awful week for me, and I know it has been awful for you too. I'm so sorry I ran away and ghosted you after you asked me to marry you. That was not the best way to handle it. I am glad, however, that I took that trip with Mandy. I needed to really consider what your offer meant and if it could work. The truth is...," she chewed at her lip again, trying to keep her emotions in check before she continued. Emma cleared her throat that now felt tight and swollen.

"The truth is that down the road, I think we might resent each other for it. There would always be this push and pull of me wanting to be in Ocala at the farm with the horses in my care, and you wanting to be here with your aunt, your job, and the rest of your world. At some point, one of us would have no other option but to move. Whoever ended up moving, well, they would be giving up what they truly wanted. I can't ask you to do that and I don't want to regret giving up a career I worked so hard for either. We are just getting started in life and I see how much you love this job. I won't be the one who asks you to move to Ocala just for me. There is nothing for you there, you said so yourself once. Liam, I'm sorry, but I can't marry you," Emma said, her eyes meeting his again as she searched them, hoping he understood.

Liam seemed to consider what she said for a moment. Maybe he was realizing what she had, that no matter how much they cared for one another, that they would still be holding each other back.

"And you are sure about this?" Liam asked, his voice sounding like he was holding back his own emotions.

"I'm sure," Emma said, conveying this with her eyes the best she could.

"I'll tell Aunt Cathy so you don't have to," Liam said.

"Thank you," Emma replied, grateful he had even offered. That was another conversation she was dreading.

"So, this is it then. For real this time," Liam said, scanning her face, as if he was trying to wrap his mind around the fact that they would not be seeing each other for a very, very long time. Since Cathy came up to the farm, really, there was no other reason for them to be in the same room after this moment. Indefinitely.

That reality hadn't quite dawned on Emma until now. She had been so worried about the awkwardness and possible strain on her working relationship with

Cathy after turning down his proposal that she hadn't considered this fact as heavily.

This *was* truly goodbye for her and Liam. For good.

"I guess it is," Emma replied softly, the sadness of this moment taking over the pressure of the impending conversation. "Maybe we can be friends?" Emma added, although she had a feeling she already knew the answer to this question.

"Em, I don't think I could be *just* friends with you," Liam said, his eyes looking away from her now.

"Ok...," she replied, trailing off, not sure what else to say. And that made this all worse.

"I'm sorry to cut this short, but I really have to get to work," Liam said, after briefly glancing at his watch.

"I understand," she stated quietly.

What else could be said at this point anyway? She had rejected him, and he wanted to move on. It was that simple.

Liam put both hands on either side of her shoulders, looking her in the eyes once more.

"Take care, Emma Walker," he said dejectedly.

"You too, Liam," Emma replied as they still stood there, eyes locked.

Liam quickly kissed her on the forehead before heading back into Cathy's estate.

Emma stood there, watching him walk away from her. The tears that had been threatening to fall for some time now finally came pouring out.

She didn't know how long she had been standing there, staring at the front door of his estate that she would probably never see the inside of again. That seemed strange to her for some reason.

Emma turned and walked to her car before Liam came back out to leave for work. That would be even more awkward, and it was best to leave now, the way they had ended it.

"It's really over," she thought, as she put her car in reverse, backing out of the driveway.

Emma drove down the familiar road, and for a moment she considered simply hopping back on the freeway towards Ocala. At least, that had been her original plan when she drove down this morning.

But now, she was feeling a little nostalgic, especially with ending things with Liam for good.

Emma pulled through the gates of Palm Beach Equestrian Center. How long had it been since she was here last? She hadn't been back at these show grounds since her last day here as a working student for Twin Oaks.

It was still somewhat of the off season for this area, but it appeared there were still some horses schooling here already. Emma parked in what used to be the parking lot closest to the Twin Oaks stalls. She wandered down the barn aisles, reminiscing about her time in this tropical, horse-filled wonderland.

The palm trees blew softly in the light breeze as she walked down the shaded path. It wasn't long before she was in the very spot where she had run into Liam.

"Hey horse girl," his words echoed through her thoughts as she remembered that moment.

How had so much changed in less than a year?

Emma continued down the path until she reached the edge of the horse show grounds to the very spot where she and Valentine had made their great escape when Bo had chased her on his motorcycle.

Emma found a quiet spot shaded by palm trees and slumped against it as she continued to reminisce. Her eyes followed the road leading down towards the horse farm neighborhood she had taken refuge in that night. It seemed so surreal now, and it was hard to believe it had actually happened to her.

Emma remembered the sound of Michael's voice when she called from that groom's phone. He had been so worried about her and dropped everything to hook up the Twin Oaks truck and trailer to get them, no questions asked. Looking back, Emma realized he probably could have been in a lot of trouble for that whole situation. Not to mention the truck and trailer crashed on his watch. Still, his only concern seemed to be her safety.

"Michael," Emma whispered aloud sweetly.

That was the real reason she was here, wasn't it? Emma had to end things with Liam before she could truly be with Michael.

"Choose the person who is like your best friend. Who can you not live without?" Mandy's words rang in her ears, as if she was right there speaking them to her.

Emma had sat on the beach that night with Mandy looking out over the dark ocean water as she had contemplated Mandy's mother's wise words.

It had come down to who she couldn't live her life without since she knew whoever she didn't choose would not be a part of her life any longer, given the circumstances. The more she thought about who she couldn't live without, the clearer her choice became.

It was Michael. Maybe for a long time it had been Michael. He *was* her best friend already. Then, when she kissed him, it was like an electric shock ran through her body. It was the spark that had been waiting to be lit.

After he had confessed his feelings for her the day they rescued Mandy from that cabin in the woods, it felt like every piece had fallen into place between them.

Had Liam never proposed, she had wondered if she would have had any doubts about her relationship with Michael. Sure, she wanted to take things slow and even now, Emma still had that in the back of her mind.

But in reality, there was no one she wanted more in her life than Michael. And that was something that had been true for a very long time now.

Emma sighed as she stood up and brushed the grass from her legs.

The hard part was finally over. Now, maybe it was time to move forward with her life.

And, with Michael.

ele

When Emma had returned back from Wellington yesterday, she was a little relieved to find the barn empty and quiet.

It was right around 8:00 pm when she had arrived back in Ocala, and even Michael was inside for the night.

Emma had figured since she had driven all that way, that she may as well make a day of it. After calling up one of her old friends that she met when she worked in Wellington, the two met up and spent the day together. A couple other mutual friends had joined them later in the day as well.

It had been so nice to see her long lost girlfriends and talk about nothing but horses for hours. If that wasn't a good palate cleanser after that morning's heartbreaking conversation with Liam, she didn't know what was.

Emma had considered knocking on Michael's door and talking to him about, well, everything. After all, they still had not spoken since she left for the coast over a week ago. A pang of guilt had ripped through her at the thought of leaving him so suddenly with him wondering how she felt.

Emma also wondered if word about the proposal had somehow gotten out. Mandy and Liam were the only people who were aware of it, as far as she knew. Still, Michael wasn't stupid. He had to suspect something serious had occurred during her conversation with Liam since it had sent her across the state without a word.

She made the decision to talk to Michael about it all after work today, and not spring it on him late last night. Besides, she wanted to sleep on it and clear her mind of the breakup with Liam before going all in with Michael. Emma was still mentally processing it all herself.

That is, until Mandy reminded her that this morning was her last day in town.

"Shoot!" Emma thought. She didn't know the next time she would see Mandy, so that meant her talk with Michael would have to wait another day.

After having breakfast with Mandy, Emma headed out to the barn.

Sliding the barn door open, Emma watched as horse heads popped out from their stalls, giving her low, excited nickers, their eyes wide.

While she could really never get sick of the beach, she had to admit, she had missed the horses. Especially Valentine. Beelining for her mare's stall, she placed two hands on either side of her mare's muzzle and kissed her velvety nose.

"How has my girl been?" Emma asked affectionately as she scratched her horse's neck. Valentine leaned into her owner's hand and nosed her chest.

"I missed you too," Emma replied to her horse's unspoken words.

It felt good to be back to normal. Between Mandy getting kidnapped and then running off to the gulf coast, this was her first normal day in weeks.

Emma was excited to get back on her own horse as well as the others she had on her list to ride today. A creaking sound came from above her head, followed by a door shutting and footsteps on the stairs.

"Michael," she thought, knowing he would be in the barn within seconds. Butterflies danced in her stomach when she thought about seeing him for the first time in so long. He had no idea what she had been thinking about all week, or that she had chosen him in the end.

Butterflies suddenly turned to anxiety. What if he was angry with her for running off like she did without even talking to him? Emma felt bad about it, looking back. It had been a cowardly thing to do. She should have told him what was going on. But even if she had, wouldn't that have been worse somehow? She imagined him sitting in his apartment alone, wondering if she would choose him or Liam, knowing he cared so deeply about her and had for some time.

What should she say to him now? Should she simply apologize and leave it at that? Emma didn't want to have a long discussion about everything that had gone on and her feelings for him in the middle of work, especially since Sam would be here any minute. It was definitely an off-the-clock type of conversation.

The barn door slid open slowly. Emma was still halfway down the barn aisle and the sun behind him made it hard to make out his expression. How mad was he? Or hurt?

"Emma?" Michael said, his tone giving away his surprise to see her back. She still couldn't see his face very well in the lighting at the end of the barn aisle.

"Hey Michael," Emma replied softly. She was dying to know how he felt. She took a few steps toward him, just enough so that she could finally read his expression.

His eyes were bunched together in confusion, mixed with a little sadness, under his worn ball cap. He tilted his head slightly, scanning her face as well, as if he was hoping to find some answers there.

"How are you?" she added before he spoke again.

He paused a moment, considering what to say next.

"I'm ok, just a little confused I guess," he replied.

Fair enough. He had every right to be.

"I'm sure you are, and I'm so sorry about that," Emma replied, wishing she could simply rush over and wrap her arms around him, but she held back.

Michael cleared his throat and shifted his weight. He didn't seem to know what to say. He seemed to be walking on eggshells around her. What did he know?

"Did you have a nice trip?" he asked awkwardly.

"I did. It gave me a lot of time to think," Emma replied. She instantly wished she hadn't said that; it was only going to make him wonder more about what was going on, and she wasn't able to give him those answers right this second.

Before either of them could say anything else, they heard a truck door shut and footsteps behind them.

"Emma, you're back!" Sam said a few seconds later as he walked through the barn doors.

"Hey Sam!" Emma said, a little glad he had interrupted the awkward conversation.

"How was the gulf coast?" he asked in a friendly tone. At least one person wasn't upset about her disappearance.

"Absolutely breathtaking. Thank you so much again for helping take care of the horses for me while I was away."

"My pleasure, ma'am," Sam said, his southern draw coming out a little bit more this time.

Sam headed toward where the wheelbarrows were stored to begin his daily chores.

Emma and Michael exchanged a quick, uncomfortable look. They both knew they would have to go about their day like nothing was wrong until they had a chance to talk during non-working hours.

Buzz let out a sharp whinny, reminding Emma she had spent enough time socializing and that he was hungry. Low nickers and whinnies echoed in the barn as the other horses chimed in with their opinions.

"Alright guys, I know, it's breakfast time," Emma said with a laugh, turning her attention back to the horses.

After they had grain and hay, Emma went back to her list in the feed room where she had left it and tried to decide which horse she wanted to work first.

"Emma?" A female voice called down the barn aisle. Emma peeked around the corner of the feed room.

Clara was walking down the aisle, clearly looking for her.

"Hey Clara!" Emma said, emerging from the feed room.

"I'm so glad you're back! Did you have a good trip? Sam and Michael mentioned you went on an impromptu girl's trip?"

Well, technically that was true.

"Yes, we did! We ended up near Clearwater, on Treasure Island, thanks for asking," Emma replied. She wasn't sure how much she should dump on Clara about her messy personal life and the reason she really went on that trip. After all, she was still getting to know Clara.

"I'm going to work Cujo if you want to ride with me?" Clara offered.

Emma remembered Clara offering to ride together before, but between Mandy being kidnapped and then her own personal drama, that simply hadn't happened yet. Emma checked her watch; it was still early. She could easily ride Valentine now with Clara, instead of later like she planned, and get the rest of the horses worked in plenty of time.

"I'd like that! Let's do it," Emma said, smiling at Clara warmly.

Truth be told, she could use a ride with a friend anyway.

They two young women tacked up quickly and mounted up shortly after.

"Want to go do some cross country schooling?" Clara asked Emma, a glimmer of excitement in her eyes.

"Definitely," Emma said. She and Valentine were always down for some galloping and jumping.

"How is Mandy doing after everything that happened to her?" Clara asked, seeming genuinely concerned about her. Emma looked over, catching the look on her face. Clara was not only sweet but seemed like a sincerely good person. Emma hoped this was the beginning of a true friendship between them. Other than Lily, she had no other girl friends in Ocala, and Emma could already tell Clara was the kind of person she could see being friends with.

"Mandy is a tough cookie," Emma said, chuckling a little as she shook her head. "She was pretty bruised and banged up, but after a few days, Mandy said she wasn't really in much pain and the bruises looked worse than they felt. I was impressed though, she never lost her sense of humor. Even being kidnapped for a few days couldn't break that girl," she said, laughing again.

"I'm so glad," Clara replied, looking relieved.

"Thank you again for working some of the horses for us while we were looking for her," Emma said.

"Of course, I was happy to help," Clara replied.

They plodded along silently after that, enjoying the cooler morning air as they headed toward the cross country field.

"Want to play a game?" Clara's blue eyes sparkled when she spoke, and her face lit up like she had just thought of a great idea.

"Sure!" Emma said, smiling too.

"I'll just start galloping around and you and Valentine can follow me? Maybe I could take him over some of the bigger stuff and your horse will feel more confident following behind him? We do this at the farm I'm a working student at sometimes with the younger, greener horses to help build confidence over bigger, scarier cross country stuff," Clara said.

"That sounds like fun!" Emma replied, excited at the thought of testing the waters of higher cross country jumps. Valentine was brave, but seeing some of those solid, massive tables coming at her at an open gallop seemed incredibly intimidating to Emma.

They both hacked across the open part of the field at a walk, trot, then canter as they warmed up. Clara then halted in front of her, and Emma followed suit.

"Ready?" Clara asked, turning around in her saddle.

"Go easy on me at first!" Emma said, tossing her a slightly concerned look.

"Don't worry, we will hit all the low jumps first and then take a quick break before we go for the big stuff," Clara replied, winking at her.

Emma nodded moments before Clara asked Cujo to canter. Clara headed in the direction of a few scattered beginner novice height jumps. She landed off one and turned toward the novice height ones, taking two before she asked Cujo to walk again and Emma brought Valentine back to a walk as well. Clara tossed Emma a playful look.

"Time to put your big girl pants on!" Clara said to Emma with a wink. Emma swallowed hard, mentally preparing herself.

Emma patted Valentine's neck, remembering the trust she had in this little mare. The memory of Valentine jumping an almost four-foot gate when they were being chased by Bo crossed her mind. If she could do that, she could do anything, including jumping these enormous looking cross country jumps.

Clara and Cujo cantered off again, this time towards the cluster of the larger jumps.

Emma found a nice balance in the saddle, focusing on keeping Valentine in front of her leg as they cantered forward.

Emma watched as Cujo leaped over the training level height table a few strides in front of them. Valentine picked up her pace, eager to stay close behind Cujo. She locked on to the table, launching over it. Emma felt the seconds tick by as they stayed airborne for longer than she was used to, and they landed on the other side at a nice open gallop. A grin stretched across her face. There was something about feeling the power of her horse under her when they jumped larger fences that always took her breath away a little bit.

Cujo was galloping towards a training level sized corner now and floated over it like the pro he was. It seemed like nothing to him, or Clara for that matter.

Emma focused on keeping her horse balanced as she eyed the perfect distance and narrowest part of the jump. Valentine ate up the ground beneath them, charging it down a little more than she had the first jump. She cleared it, leaving a little room to spare. Emma beamed again, wondering just how much scope this little mare had in her. So far, it looked like they could jump just about anything they put their minds to.

After two more training level sized jumps, Clara slowed to a trot and then walk again, smiling as she turned around in the saddle to meet Emma's gaze. Emma still had a smile plastered on her face.

"Pretty fun, huh?" Clara asked.

"That was awesome," Emma said breathlessly.

Emma and Clara walked their horses toward the shaded portion of the field to catch their breath.

"I know we don't know each other very well, but can I ask...what's the deal with you and Michael?" Clara asked, looking over and then immediately dropping her gaze. She seemed shy about asking, but curious enough to do so anyway.

Emma paused, caught off guard a little by Clara's question.

"I'm sorry, I don't mean to pry, and you don't have to answer if you're not comfortable. It's just...well, when you were gone, he seemed pretty beat up about it. I don't exactly know why Liam came at Michael the way he did at the grand opening party, but my guess is it has something to do with his feelings for you," Clara added quickly, noticing Emma's hesitation to answer.

Was it that obvious to everyone around them? Of course, the incident at the party had been a pretty clear indication. But now she knew; Michael had been miserable while she was away. That made her stomach churn; the last thing she wanted was to hurt Michael.

Emma sighed and looked over at Clara with a weak smile.

"It's kind of a long story," Emma began. She filled Clara in on her and Michael's backstory, telling her about the kiss the night of the Million Dollar Grand Prix and that it was the reason Liam had done what he did to Michael at the Grand Opening party. She briefed her on how they kissed again, and how he confessed his feelings for her less than twenty-four hours before Liam's proposal.

Clara's jaw dropped at that part, but she snapped it shut quickly, her eyes flitting away. Clara seemed to not want to be rude about her reaction.

"So that's why I ran off and why Michael was acting the way he was. Just yesterday I told Liam in person I couldn't marry him. Now, I just need to talk to Michael," Emma said, wrapping up the story.

"Wow," Clara said. She seemed to be looking for the right words to say as they continued walking along. "I can see why you picked him though. Michael seems like a great guy, and he clearly cares about you," Clara replied, her eyes meeting Emma's again.

"He is the best guy I know," Emma replied, almost at a whisper.

She had to admit, it was nice being able to talk through everything with someone who didn't know her very well. If even Clara could see what was between them, maybe Emma truly had made the right choice after all.

It was comforting, considering how guilt ridden she still felt about hurting Liam the way she had.

Chapter Three

Emma felt a flutter of nerves rip through her as she saw Cathy's car pull into the driveway just outside the barn doors.

Sure, she was excited to meet the trainer that Cathy was all but ready to hire. However, she had not seen or talked to Cathy since she turned down Liam's proposal. Emma knew her decision to end things with Liam for good would surely put a strain on her working relationship with Cathy, but that didn't mean she was looking forward to the fall out.

Emma sighed audibly, putting down the broom she had been using to re-sweep the aisleway so it looked perfect for today's visitor.

Yesterday, Emma had had a bittersweet final evening with Mandy. She still couldn't believe her friend was back to traveling for work and not sitting in the house on her laptop like Emma had become accustomed to. Still, the few weeks she had been able to spend with her best friend in town couldn't have been timed any better, minus the whole kidnapping thing, of course. Mandy had been here right when she needed her though, and for that Emma was grateful.

But with Mandy gone, she now had to face the fallout of recent events involving Liam and Michael on her own. And that was definitely not something Emma was looking forward to.

"Hi Cathy," Emma said as she plastered a smile on her face when Cathy walked into the barn.

"Emma, how are you dear?" Cathy replied with a smile. Cathy's usual enthusiasm didn't ring in her words, but otherwise, she seemed to be acting normally. That was a relief.

"Looking forward to meeting this trainer you have told me so much about! You said you know her already?" Emma asked, pressing for the details Cathy had not yet shared about this potential trainer for Live Oaks Farm.

"Oh yes, Bree Lawson and I go way back," Cathy said, seeming to reminisce as she spoke. "Bree was the up-and-coming young rider that was dominating the leaderboards at every competition we both attended. We started off as competitors, but eventually, we became friends. She moved up north to Maryland for a while, but she has since been looking to move back to Ocala for some time now. When a mutual friend of ours mentioned she was looking for a training job down here, I called her right away," Cathy added, looking proud of her meddling.

Emma was glad Cathy had found someone she seemed to trust and know already. They had been hitting one dead end after another when it came to hiring a trainer. She and Cathy had both wondered if they were ever going to find someone that was the right fit for them. Now, it seemed like they finally had.

"Ah, there she is!" Cathy said, clasping her hands together.

A tall, slender woman who appeared to be in her mid-forties with dirty blonde colored hair stepped out of the truck. A smile spread across her face when she caught sight of Cathy in the doorway of the barn.

"Cathy! Is that you? You haven't aged a day! It has been too long," Bree said with enthusiasm that reminded Emma a little bit of Cathy's. They two women embraced for a long moment before stepping back to look at each other, smiling. It made sense why these two had formed a friendship years ago; they were two peas in a pod.

"Bree, this is Live Oak's barn manager, Emma. Emma this is my dear friend Bree," Cathy said.

"It's so nice to meet you, Bree. Cathy has had so many wonderful things to say about you," Emma said, shaking the woman's hand.

"Oh has she now? Well, I hope she mentioned how I used to win against her back in the day," Bree said with a wink at Cathy.

"Only half the time," Cathy rebutted with a laugh.

Cathy led the way into the barn as she showed Bree around. They toured the entire property and made their way back to the front of the barn when they had finished.

"Cathy, this place is stunning," Bree said, tossing Cathy a genuine smile. "Have you started adding to your young horse project stock yet?" Bree added.

"No, not yet. Emma and I hadn't had much luck finding a trainer that was the right fit for us, so we held off buying young, farm-owned project horses until we did," Cathy replied.

"Well, then it looks like you two will get to finally go horse shopping then! If you will have me that is," Bree said, looking at Cathy with a warm smile.

"We would be honored to have you," Cathy replied, placing her hand on Bree's shoulder.

"Welcome to the Live Oaks team!" Emma added.

Cathy and Emma spent some time discussing a start date and schedule with Bree. Bree said she could be moved and begin work within two weeks. And just like that, the farm was officially fully staffed.

Cathy waved as Bree got in her truck and headed out of the black iron gates towards to road. Cathy turned around and looked at Emma with a satisfied expression.

"I think she will make a wonderful addition to the team," Emma said.

"You know, Bree was right about one thing," Cathy said, a little mischief in her eyes.

"What's that?"

"We get to go horse shopping," Cathy stated.

Cathy turned around as she headed toward her car without another word.

"Where is she going?" Emma thought.

"Are you coming?" Cathy said, suddenly turning around.

Emma paused, unsure what she meant. "Where?"

"Horse shopping of course!" Cathy said before opening her driver's side door.

"Now?" Emma thought.

Emma jogged over to the passenger door of Cathy's vehicle, sliding into the leather seat.

"Where are we going to horse shop, exactly?" Emma asked, eyeing Cathy curiously. After all, normally these things required appointments.

"Oh, I have a couple things set up. I figured today's interview would go well," Cathy replied, winking at Emma.

Leave it to Cathy. It didn't surprise Emma that Cathy had pre-planned this. It made sense though since Cathy was only planning to be in town today and heading back to Wellington in the morning.

Emma wondered if Cathy would bring up Emma's turning down of Liam's proposal. Emma still felt the weight of that hanging over her head. In the silence as they drove, she almost opened her mouth twice to say something but clamped it shut each time. What exactly could she say? Sorry I didn't love your nephew back and decided to be with someone else despite the fact you have done so much for me? All her words fell flat in her mind, and none of them made enough sense to actually speak.

They pulled into the long driveway of a farm that made Emma's jaw drop down a little. It was almost equally as impressive as Three Phases Farm and its stunning grounds took her breath away.

They parked near the largest barn on the property, and a middle-aged man in khakis and a polo stepped out of the barn to greet them.

"Cathy, love! You look radiant as always," the man gushed as they embraced. Did Cathy know everyone important in Ocala? It certainly seemed like it.

"Stop it Charles, you're too much," Cathy replied as she gently swatted his shoulder. Cathy turned her attention back to Emma.

"Charles, this is my barn manager, Emma," Cathy said, motioning towards her.

Charles stretched his hand out to shake hers.

"A pleasure, Emma," he said, smiling warmly as they shook hands.

"Charles is well known for breeding some of the nicest eventing horses I've encountered over the years," Cathy said as Charles led them into the impressive looking barn.

Emma's eyes widened as she peered into every stall. Each one contained a young horse, all looking between the ages of two and four. Their coats shined with health and one look at their conformation told Emma these horses were bred for one thing: eventing.

"What breeds are they?" Emma asked breathlessly, feeling like a kid being led through a toy store as they continued on down the aisle.

"Warmbloods. We like to add a lot of Thoroughbred to our bloodlines though; we find it really gives them that heart and endurance that makes a good upper level horse," Charles replied.

"Mostly Charles likes the Irish Sport Horses and Trakehners, but he also has some Dutch Warmbloods in his stock," Cathy added.

"Right this way," Charles said as he motioned toward the entrance of the indoor arena at the end of the aisle.

Emma saw several grooms holding the reins to four young horses. They looked like they could gallop at a three-foot fence right now and jump it with ease based on the way they were built.

"These are the youngsters I pulled for you to look at based on your criteria, Cathy," Charles said, as they approached the young horses.

Emma couldn't help herself and ran her hand up the forelock of a black filly.

"Emma loves the mares," Cathy commented to Charles.

"She has good taste! I've always had a soft spot for the mares. It's how I got into the breeding business in the first place," Charles replied, shooting Emma an endearing look.

Charles had the grooms jog the horses in front of Emma and Cathy, and then sent them through the jumping chute one by one. Emma resisted to urge to ooh and ahh out loud as the fillies and colts floated effortlessly over the jumps.

Cathy pointed out her top two favorites of the four-year-old horses, and Charles sent them to be saddled. The grooms returned a few minutes later with the two young horses fully tacked up.

The groom walked one of the two horses over to the mounting block and looked directly at Emma. Emma paused, shooting a surprised look at Cathy.

"Go on," Cathy said, shooing her toward the filly with a smirk. Emma beamed as she walked toward the young horse, taking the helmet from the groom who was handing it to her. It was a good thing she was already in breeches and boots, the by-products of working on a horse farm.

Emma swung a leg over the filly's back, settling gently in the saddle. She gingerly asked her to walk forward and lapped the arena as she got a feel for the unfamiliar horse beneath her.

Asking for the trot now, Emma was surprised at how smooth her gaits were. It reminded her a little of that lazy-boy type ride her own horse had. But with breeding like this, it was really no surprise.

The filly floated along under her and Emma began testing her to see what she knew. It surprised her how responsive and soft in the bridle the filly was. It was clear she had been professionally trained from the ground up. Emma asked for a canter after sufficiently warming up at the trot and found it equally as comfortable as the two previous gaits. Her canter was naturally uphill, the kind that would be perfect for approaching a jump.

"Take her over that cross rail," Charles instructed, pointing it out.

Emma wrapped her legs around the filly as she found a nice rhythm, pointing her to the jump. The filly jumped in a nice round frame without hesitation, and landed in the same, soft three beat canter she left the ground with. Emma smiled widely, bringing her back to the walk.

"She's perfect," Emma said, looking over at Cathy.

"Good! Let's have her try the colt too," Cathy said, nodding.

Emma dismounted the filly and headed back over to the mounting block where a groom had the colt ready to go. Emma found the colt had similar, comfortable gaits, although not quite as smooth as the filly. His had a little bit more bounce. Still, he responded to her every aid exceptionally well for his age, and it was clear he had a very easy-going nature about him.

Emma hopped off the colt, looking over at Cathy again. "He's lovely, such an easy ride for a young horse," Emma said, looking over at Charles with an impressed look. His young horses were as well-mannered as they were stunning to look at. Emma was afraid to ask how much they cost; she was sure they were expensive.

"I would love to take them both, Charles. I can send Michael over to pick them up tomorrow if that's ok? I can have the payment sent over this afternoon," Cathy said with an excited look in her eyes.

"Wonderful! I will have my staff get everything ready for them to haul out tomorrow," Charles replied, shaking Cathy's hand.

Live Oaks now had their first farm-owned sale prospects. Emma was excited to help Bree bring them along and ride such nice horses. Their caliber was obvious, and Emma felt pride swell inside of her that she could be a part of their training and care.

Charles led the way back through the barn, chatting excitedly with Cathy about her new horses.

"We have to run to our next appointment dear, but it was lovely seeing you again Charles," Cathy said to him. Then she turned to Emma.

"Emma dear, will you please be sure to set time aside in your schedule tomorrow to help Michael pick up these horses? I want to make sure you get a chance to talk to Charles' staff so you get every bit of information about them and their routine so they transition well."

"Of course!" Emma said, excited for the opportunity to come back to this stunning farm one more time. But excitement was quickly washed away by anxiety. She still hadn't talked to Michael in depth. Emma knew from her and Clara's conversation that he had been pretty upset while she was away, which wasn't a great sign. Stuck in a truck together tomorrow would be awkward if she didn't get a chance to talk to him prior, but based on how today was going, it didn't look like they were going to be back at the farm until late. The more days that passed, the more Emma dreaded the conversation with Michael. The thought of admitting to him Liam had proposed and that she had run away to essentially choose between them made her sick to her stomach.

Cathy thanked Charles again for taking the time to meet with them today and he congratulated her once more on her purchases.

They got back in Cathy's car and headed down the back road that led to the main road. Emma wondered where they were going next but decided not to ask; it was kind of fun letting it stay a surprise.

Cathy pulled into the driveway of a much different looking farm this time. While everything about the last farm screamed high class breeding operation, this one had a much humbler appearance. In fact, at first she wondered why they were even at a farm like this. Not that she cared. Emma grew up riding in much humbler, smaller-scale barns. But it just seemed to be a glaring difference from the type of facility they had just visited and purchased horses from. Emma's curiosity peaked as they rounded the corner and headed to the worn-looking white barn.

Then, Emma caught a white, racetrack type railing out of the corner of her eye. Emma spun around quickly in her seat as she looked over at Cathy.

"Is this what I think it is?" Emma asked, a smile breaking over her face now.

"If you mean a Thoroughbred farm, then yes, it is," Cathy replied, looking pleased with herself. Emma hopped out of the car the moment Cathy put it in park. Her eyes scanned the miles of rolling hills dotted with horses. A horse that had been on the far side of the track before now galloped past the railing closest to them, its hooves pounding against the dirt.

Emma's eyes widened as she took it all in. Her first horse, Lexington, had been an off-the-track Thoroughbred. Not only that, but Maggie had pulled countless horses from the track to retrain, and Emma had grown up riding so many of these lovely horses. They had a very special place in her heart.

A woman with dark brown hair pulled into a ponytail emerged from the barn. She was short and slender, and if Emma had to guess, she was probably an exercise rider.

"You must be Cathy," the woman said, shaking her hand.

"Leanne, I presume?" Cathy replied with a warm smile.

"Yes. Dave had so many nice things to say about you. Please, right this way," Leanne said, ushering them into the barn.

"Dave is retired now, and Leanne, his longtime exercise rider and assistant trainer, is showing us a few horses today," Cathy said in a low voice as they walked a little way behind Leanne.

Emma couldn't stop smiling. She had always liked Cathy for her love of horses, and she didn't blame her one bit for wanting the nicely bred horses they had already purchased, but Emma felt an even deeper sense of admiration for Cathy as they headed towards the two Thoroughbreds standing in cross-ties across from each other. Cathy could afford to buy all well-bred young stock if she wanted, but here she was about to purchase ex-racehorses. Emma wondered if she was simply doing it for her sake or if she truly loved the off-the-track thoroughbreds the way Emma did. She had never really thought to ask.

Cathy stroked the neck of a tall, dark bay gelding. "He looks a lot like my junior horse did," Cathy said affectionately. Ah, so perhaps she had a Thoroughbred growing up?

"Dave mentioned you bought one of his horses years ago, was that your junior horse?" Leanne asked, all but answering Emma's unspoken questions.

"Yes. Although, he wasn't the only horse that I bought from Dave," Cathy replied, still running her hand along the gelding's smooth coat.

"How many off-the-track Thoroughbreds have you had?" Emma asked, curious now.

"Oh my, quite a few over the years. Most of the horses I rode in my younger years were Thoroughbreds," Cathy replied.

It all made sense now.

Leanne had the groom jog both horses that Dave had hand selected for Cathy.

"How long have they been off-the-track?" Cathy asked Leanne.

"Both raced about a month ago. Dave said these two had a lot of qualities you'd like in an eventing mount," Leanne replied.

Cathy looked both of the horses up and down again, her eyes passing over their conformation.

"They certainly do," Cathy agreed. "Could we pick them up tomorrow?"

"Of course, I will let Dave know and get them ready for you," Leanne replied with a smile.

Emma was a little surprised at how quickly Cathy decided on purchasing the two Thoroughbreds. After all, they hadn't sat on either of them. Although, she imagined these horses were incredibly inexpensive compared to the well-bred Warmbloods they had purchased. Plus, it seemed she had a very long-term relationship with this farm's owner and Leanne said he had hand selected these two in particular.

"Emma, I will be sure to write down both farm's addresses for you and Michael," Cathy said, turning to her.

It looked like she and Michael would certainly be spending some extended forced alone time together tomorrow. Emma gulped, thinking once again about that impending conversation.

"Thank you for your help, dear, and please pass along my thanks to Dave. I hope he is doing well," Cathy said.

"Oh yes, he is doing a lot more golfing these days. He still likes to be involved with the farm's operations, but just isn't working in the barns as hands-on as he used to. He says he is getting too old for that kind of thing," Leanne replied with a chuckle, shaking her head.

"Well I'm glad to hear he is enjoying retirement," Cathy said as they headed back toward her car.

"See you tomorrow, Emma!" Leanne said with a wave before disappearing back into the barn.

"Nice meeting you!" Emma called back as she walked away.

Cathy's car bumped down the gravel road as they headed back to Live Oak's Farm. Emma had learned a little something about Cathy today that made her love her more than she already did. Emma recalled when she first met Cathy how she commented about Emma reminded her of herself when she was younger. Emma was beginning to see just how true that really was. Perhaps that could be enough to help move them past the awkwardness of her breakup with Liam.

Before Emma could talk herself out of it, she decided to rip off the band-aid.

"I'm sorry about what happened between Liam and I," Emma said, he eyes dropping to the floor of the car.

Cathy glanced over at her briefly, a surprised look on her face. She probably wasn't expecting Emma to come right out and say that after not mentioning it all day.

"How is he?" Emma added quickly, meeting Cathy's gaze again.

A sad half smile crossed Cathy's face.

"He's not quite himself these days, but he will be ok. And there is no need to be sorry. I want you to be happy, no matter who that you end up with," Cathy replied.

It was clear she was implying that if she wanted to be with Michael, Cathy wasn't going to hold that against her. At least, that's what Emma hoped she meant.

"Do you love him?" Cathy added before Emma had a chance to reply.

Emma was caught off guard. She had not expected Cathy to say something quite like that about Michael.

"I...er...no. I don't think so. Not yet anyway." Emma's cheeks flushed red, and her gaze returned to the car's floorboard.

"I haven't talked to him about it yet. He doesn't even know..." Emma trailed off, biting her lip. This was an awkward conversation to have with your ex-boyfriend's aunt.

"Dear, if I may offer some advice?"

Emma nodded, not looking up.

"Time flies. One minute you are twenty-something and then you blink and you are my age. If you care about someone, don't waste too much time letting them think otherwise."

Emma looked up again, seeing the wisdom in Cathy's eyes. She was right. If she had made her decision, why was she using every excuse in the book to not talk to Michael?

"Thanks Cathy," Emma replied, trying her best to let her expression convey how much she appreciated her.

At least now she knew Cathy didn't hate her for rejecting Liam.

Now, she just had to hope Michael still felt the same way about her after everything that had happened.

Emma heard the sound of the empty trailer rattling, getting louder as it approached the open barn doors.

A small wave of nerves hit her as she walked down the barn aisle towards the truck and trailer waiting for her outside. While she was excited to go pick up the new horses Cathy purchased, she still had mixed feelings about the conversation she knew she would soon be having with Michael.

The last few days had been so busy between Mandy leaving, hiring Bree, and horse shopping. Emma had managed to all but avoid seeing Michael since that awkward moment they shared in the barn after she had returned home from her trip.

But today, stuck in a truck for what she assumed would be at least several hours, there would be no excuse. And that is what had her stomach in knots. What exactly would he say when she confessed everything?

Emma pulled the truck door open, avoiding eye contact with Michael as she slid in. Keeping her gaze locked on the windshield in front of them, she tried to slow her breathing, reminding herself it probably would be best to wait until they had picked up the horses before starting any kind of deep conversation. How awkward and unprofessional would it be if she showed up to one of the farms looking like she had just been crying or visibly distressed? Emma couldn't have that be her reputation. After all, she was still establishing herself in the new role.

She could feel Michael's eyes on her. Emma turned slightly, but he looked away before she had a chance to read his expression.

Yep, it was going to be a long drive. The first farm may only be fifteen minutes away, but the time between now and the conversation she was dreading would surely feel like an eternity.

They pulled out of the farm's gates and onto the back road. The road wound around as horse farms passed by on either side. Emma kept her eyes locked on the scenery outside her passenger window. The silence in the truck hung heavy between them.

"Couldn't Michael think to turn on the radio?" she thought.

"Just make it past the horse pickups," she reminded herself. Being an emotional wreck in front of these horse professionals was not an option.

"So, uh, did you have fun horse shopping with Cathy?" Michael asked, shifting in his seat. His voice sounded like he wasn't sure what else to say. Maybe he simply wanted to break the awkward silence like she did. Could she blame him?

"It was a lot of fun; Cathy seems to know everyone in this town," Emma said, tossing a quick glance and half smile at Michael. She didn't let her eyes meet his though, and her gaze immediately returned to the passenger side window.

"That's good," he said half-heartedly. Michael cleared his throat but didn't say anything else.

They finally pulled into the driveway of the first farm she and Cathy visited yesterday. Emma quickly looked over at Michael, whose jaw had dropped slightly.

She couldn't help herself; she had to know how he would react to this stunning farm. Emma smiled to herself a little, glad she wasn't the only one who had been blown away by it.

Emma hopped out of the truck the minute it was in park, partly because you could cut the tension with a knife in that truck cab, and partly because she was excited to collect their new fancy young horses. Cathy had tasked her with naming the two horses they were picking up from this farm today. The two ex-racehorses already had barn names, and while Cathy had mentioned she could change them if she wanted, Emma liked the idea of letting those horses keep the names they were used to.

Emma could hear Michael's boots on the concrete following a little way behind her. She didn't turn around and beelined for the barn's office where she had been instructed to go.

"Hello, I'm Emma Walker. I'm here to pick up the two horses we purchased yesterday?"

The slender man sitting at the dark wood desk stood, ushering her in the direction of the horses.

"Right this way," he said.

Emma accidentally made eye contact with Michael as she walked into the barn aisle. She dropped her gaze to the floor, wishing she hadn't seen the look in his green eyes.

Michael trailed right behind her as they followed the barn manager around a corner.

"It's the first two stalls here," he stated, pointing them out.

"Can you please send me home with information about what food and supplements they are on?" Emma said, turning toward the man again.

"Of course, I have some paperwork back at the office for you," he replied.

Emma turned around towards Michael, who was already opening the stall closest to him.

"I'll start loading them up," he said, without meeting her eyes this time. Emma felt a little bit like she was punched in the gut.

Emma and the barn's manager went over the horses' feeding and supplements, current riding, and turnout routines, and she signed off on the necessary paperwork. By the time Emma got back to the trailer, both horses were loaded and Michael was leaning against the side of the truck, his arms folded against his chest. He was staring in the opposite direction, looking out at the nearby pasture full of mares and foals.

Emma tilted her head, looking at him. He looked handsome standing there. She shook her head; she didn't have time to stare too long for risk he would catch her.

"Ready to head out?" she asked as casually as she could manage.

"Sure," he replied, walking towards the driver's side.

"*One down, one to go,*" Emma thought.

The short drive to the next farm felt even more awkward somehow. All the unspoken words made the air feel thick, making it hard for her to breath.

She couldn't get out of the truck fast enough; this time the truck had barely come to a complete stop and wasn't even in park. Emma wondered if Michael thought she hated him, or didn't want to be friends, let alone more, with him any longer. She hoped he would forgive her when she explained everything.

Leanne, the woman she met yesterday, was waiting outside for them by the time they reached the barn.

"Nice to see you again, Emma!" she greeted her cheerfully. Emma shook off the inner turmoil and forced a smile at Leanne.

"You as well!" she said, perhaps overdoing the enthusiasm a little. Whoops.

"I have them all ready for you in the grooming bays," Leanne said with a smile in her voice. She looked ecstatic that these horses had found such a wonderful home with them. Truth be told, it always melted Emma's heart no matter how many times she bought off-the-track Thoroughbreds. Knowing they were safe and getting a chance at a second career, well, that was priceless.

"The darker bay is Kenny, and the bright bay is Rosey," Leanne said, motioning to each horse as she spoke. Emma ran her hand up Rosey's forelock, twisting her fingers through the silky strands. Then she walked over to the gelding and scratched his neck underneath his mane. They were both sleek and racing fit, but clearly well cared for. Cathy had raved about how well the owner of this farm had treated his racehorses, how they always had excellent ground manners, and were always lovely to re-train.

Even now, Emma could see that was true through the horses' mannerisms. A lot of the ex-racehorses she had worked with didn't know how to cross-tie when they first came home. Both of these horses seemed completely at ease standing there. It made her excited to start working with them; she was sure they would be fun re-training projects.

Leanne had stepped across the aisle to the barn office while Emma had been lost in thought and was now returning with their Jockey Club paperwork and some other necessary paperwork. Emma signed off for Cathy again.

Leanne looked at Rosey then over at Kenny, affectionately patting them both.

"You two be good for your new owner," she cooed. It was obvious she cared for these horses like her own. Emma hoped this was only the beginning of a business relationship with Leanne and the farm's owner.

"I will take good care of them, I promise," Emma said, offering a warm smile to Leanne. She hoped to convey just how true that was.

"I'm sure you will," Leanne replied, smiling back.

Emma unclipped Rosey first, leading her towards the trailer that was open and ready. Michael followed suit, unclipping Kenny from the cross-ties as he led him behind Emma and the mare.

Once the horses were loaded up, Emma walked back over to Leanne and gave her a hug. For some reason, she felt like she had known Leanne longer than two short visits. Perhaps their love of this beautiful, athletic breed had something to do with it.

"I'm sure we will be in touch. Cathy and I will be getting more project horses as time goes on," Emma said.

"I'm sure we will. Take care!" Leanne said, waving as Emma walked back to the truck and trailer.

Emma slid into the truck's passenger seat, feeling good about the horses in the trailer behind them. She had been so wrapped up in her thoughts about these two horses though that for a moment the impending conversation with Michael had slipped her mind.

Now, it was like someone dumped a bag of bricks on her brain. There were no excuses, no reason not to discuss the inevitable.

Emma swallowed hard. She had told herself that once the horses were in the trailer, it would be safe to open the floodgates and say what she needed to say. But now, it suddenly felt hollow having a conversation like this in a truck.

It only made sense to wait until after they were back at the farm with the horses settled into their stalls. At least, that's the reasoning she was using for delaying this conversation another twenty minutes.

Emma felt Michael's gaze shift to her, but once again she decided not to meet it. She thought she heard Michael take a breath like he was going to say something, but no words came out of his mouth.

Michael's hand reached for the volume knob as he turned up the radio. At least this time they wouldn't be driving in thick, awkward silence.

They finally pulled back through the gates of Live Oak Farms. Emma threw herself into making sure the horses' stalls were ready with flakes of hay tossed into the corners. After they were unloaded and settling into their stalls, she headed to the feed room with the paperwork and added the new horses to her feed board. Other than putting the horses' ownership paperwork in the safe in the house, she realized there was nothing else left to do. Sam was already gone, and the barn was quiet. Sam had left her note saying he fed the other horses.

So that left just one thing: talking to Michael.

Emma slowly emerged from the tack room and saw Michael sweeping the barn aisle. It was obvious it had already been swept by Sam after he fed. There had only been a little bit of hay that managed to fall from the flakes when she tossed them into the new horses' stalls and would have been fine to leave until morning.

Emma wondered if he was simply trying to keep busy. His own mind must be racing as much as hers. Maybe more so since he had absolutely no idea what was going on between them. At least she knew where they stood. That is, if Michael didn't hate her after she told him everything.

"Thanks," Emma said softly, as she slowly approached him.

Michael turned around with a look on his face that said he hadn't expected her to talk directly to him. Fair enough. She *had* been avoiding doing so all day. And, for days prior, for that matter.

"You're welcome," he replied, almost at a whisper. Emma's eyes met his. The sadness and confusion was obvious. Emma's chest tightened; she *had* hurt Michael. That was clear. But she was about to hurt him twice.

Michael dropped his gaze and turned around, heading toward the barn doors. He clearly did not expect her to say anything else.

"Michael."

He turned around slowly, looking surprised, but said nothing.

"Can we talk?" Emma asked, taking a step toward him.

"*Now* you want to talk?" his words sounded almost cold, not the Michael she was used to. She may have hurt him worse than she originally anticipated.

"Yes, er, I know I owe you an explanation," she stammered.

Michael leaned against the side of a stall; his eyes scrunched together under his ball cap.

"That's an understatement," he replied, his voice still sounding guarded.

"I'm going to tell you everything, and I hope you can forgive me when I do," she said in a softened tone. He kept his eyes locked on hers but didn't respond to that. Emma proceeded anyway.

"That day Liam showed up, after we rescued Mandy...Liam proposed," Emma said, sucking in air, and holding her breath as she waited for Michael to process that information. Michael's eyes went wide, and he shifted his weight to his other foot. Emma couldn't quite read his expression, so she waited anxiously for him to speak.

"And that's why you had Mandy tell me you were leaving for vacation?"

Emma nodded. "I know it was a cowardly thing to do. I should have told you myself."

"Were you thinking you might say yes? Is that why you couldn't face me?" Michael asked.

Emma bit her lip, knowing he wouldn't like her answer.

"I...I wasn't sure what to do," Emma stammered. She realized she wasn't exactly answering his question.

"But you were thinking about it? You considered marrying him?" Michael pressed.

Of course she had considered it. She and Liam had history, and she couldn't simply turn him down without considering all her options.

"I had a lot to consider," Emma stated, her words coming out cracked and quiet.

Michael turned around, taking two more steps towards the barn door. Emma wondered if that was the end of the conversation.

He suddenly turned back around, and to her surprise, walked straight over to her. He was only inches away from her now. Emma could see his expression perfectly now. Those green eyes that typically sparkled when they looked at her were darkened now.

"Even after what happened between us, you considered it? For a week?! You just vanished, Em," Michael replied, his eyes locked on hers, like he was searching for the answers there.

Yes, Michael was hurt. He had told her everything about how he felt. They had kissed, more than once. She had even initiated the first kiss. He felt betrayed, and Emma couldn't even blame him. The selfish way she had handled all of this had hurt both Liam and Michael. Was she about to lose them both now? What good was deciding between the two of them if she ruined things with the man she had chosen in the end? Emma internally reprimanded herself for putting this conversation off. It clearly had only made Michael feel worse.

He was still staring at her, waiting for her to say something.

Anything.

"Liam and I...we had history. It wasn't fair to him or anyone if I simply turned him down. I needed to think, Michael. I'm sorry, I'm just *so* sorry for how it all happened...," Emma began.

But Michael was turning away from her, walking back down the aisle.

"I chose you!" Emma all but shouted after him.

Michael paused but didn't turn around.

"Emma, I think I need some time," Michael replied before heading out of the barn and around the corner. She could hear the creak of him walking up the wooden stairs to his apartment.

Emma sank to her knees; her hands covered her face. Fat tears fell from her eyes.

Boy had she screwed things up big time. Maybe she assumed Michael would simply forgive her and understand the position she was in when Liam proposed. But she had clearly underestimated his feelings for her.

"I'm sorry Michael," she whimpered to herself.

It was a good thing no one was around to see her now.

Chapter Four

Emma poured her to-go coffee cup to the top. Normally she liked a little cream and sugar, but today, she kept it straight up black. She didn't want to waste the room with fillers. This was going to be one of those days where there might not be enough coffee in the world.

To say she hadn't slept well was an understatement. Falling asleep had been hard; staying asleep had been harder. Her dreams even haunted her.

Emma dreamed Michael was at the end of a very long, dark tunnel and no matter how fast or far she ran, she could never quite catch him. The nice thing about bad dreams is you can wake up and remind yourself it wasn't real.

The problem with this dream was that at its core, it was true. She very well might have lost Michael.

"For a week?! You just vanished, Em," Michael's words rang in her mind. What if she had simply stayed? Or told him what happened before she left? Would he have understood then?

Emma sighed audibly as she pushed the front door open. There was no avoiding him, and she was just going to have to hope time would mean less strain between them.

Right now though, it was hard to imagine.

Emma walked across the grass, closing her eyes while she sucked in the cool, wet morning air. This was normally her favorite time of day. Today, it was tainted.

Emma slid the barn doors open, her stomach churning as she saw Michael's figure at the end of the barn aisle.

"Good morning," Emma said, trying to sound cheerful. Instead, it came out sounding weak and sad.

"Morning," Michael replied, barely looking up from what he was doing, not making eye contact.

Yep, it was going to be an awkward day.

Emma wasted no time feeding the horses so she could move on to riding.

In fact, she was so focused on her work that she crossed off most of the horses on her riding list in record time.

The last on her list was Kenny, the off-the-track Thoroughbred they had just purchased. Emma cold-hosed Rosey, the other Thoroughbred they had purchased, with a smile. It had been a lovely ride on the green mare who had done nothing but try her little heart out, despite not understanding exactly what she was supposed to do in an arena and not a track. She could already tell what a little superstar in the making Rosey would be. Emma was excited to ride the other horse from that farm, eager to see if he was an equally pleasant ride.

"Someone is going to be done for the day early," Sam said, chuckling a little as he watched her gently place her saddle on Kenny's back. Sam patted the gelding's neck, sneaking him a treat from his pocket.

Michael walked in front of Emma and Sam, his eyes never leaving the ground in front of him. Emma could all but feel the tension between them. She wondered if Sam could feel it to.

Sam's eyes followed Michael, whose back looked stiff as he retreated. His gaze flitted back to Emma, a slight frown stretching across his face.

"Is everything ok?" Sam asked her, raising an eyebrow curiously.

Ah, so he could tell. Shoot. The last thing she wanted was to rope Sam into their drama.

"We…um," she stammered. "Sorry Sam, I hate that this is awkward for you," Emma finally spit out, not sure how much she should tell him. Emma also wasn't sure if Michael was still in earshot. Gossiping to Sam about their issues would only make things worse.

Sam placed a hand on Emma's shoulder, giving her a sympathetic look. "You guys will figure it out," Sam replied.

"Thanks Sam," Emma said, offering a thankful half smile.

Emma slipped the bridle over Kenny's ears and led him to the mounting block. Rosey had been a little wiggly when Emma asked her to stand at the mounting block but had quickly realized what her rider wanted, and Emma was finally able to swing a leg over. This was no surprise though as many of the racehorses she had helped retrain had never been mounted at a mounting block. Most racehorses are used to having a jockey thrown on their back as they walk without missing a beat.

Kenny tried to walk off several times, and Emma patiently circled him around, grabbing the outside rein as she tried to steady him. Kenny backed up this time and appeared to be getting a little nervous.

"It's ok buddy, easy," Emma murmured.

"Do you want some help?" Michael asked.

Emma's head spun around in surprise at the sound of his voice. He was standing just outside the barn with an empty wheelbarrow still in his hands. How long had he been standing there?

"Actually, that would be great, thanks," Emma said, trying to hide the surprise in her voice.

Michael set the wheelbarrow down and walked over the Kenny. He gently ran a hand down the horse's neck, trying to soothe him a moment. The horse's head slowly came down and his eyes relaxed. Emma almost forgot how naturally good Michael was with the horses. It made her want to pull him in and give him a kiss. Unfortunately, she could barely get him to look at her right now.

Michael positioned Kenny in front of the mounting block while holding his reins and murmuring "good boy" to him.

Emma reached over to the other side of the horse's side, patting his barrel. She then gingerly put a foot in the stirrup and slowly began to swing her leg over until she placed her foot in the other stirrup.

Kenny didn't move this time, distracted by Michael's affection and voice.

"Good boy, Kenny!" Emma said, smiling as he patted his neck.

Michael's head tilted back, and his eyes briefly held hers before he looked away. He still wasn't looking at her the way he used to, but at least this time his expression looked less cold.

"Thank you," Emma said barely above a whisper.

"You're welcome," Michael replied before heading back to his abandoned wheel-barrow.

Emma clucked to Kenny, gently squeezing his sides with her legs. Kenny walked off quietly, seeming completely fine now that the mounting block issue was behind him.

After they had lapped the arena at the walk a few times, she decided to see how would be at the trot. He trotted off at a quick pace, and Emma used her seat to slow him down. By the time they had circled once more around the ring, he was offering a fairly consistent pace.

Emma brought him back to the walk, praising him and smiling as she did. She had to admit, it felt good to be working with young, off-the-track Thoroughbreds again. It reminded her of her younger years helping Maggie at her barn.

Emma hacked Kenny out of the arena and into one of the pastures. His ears swiveled as he took in the new scenery, but he plodded along rather calmly.

Sighing, she thought about her moment with Michael.

She could only hope he wouldn't hate her forever.

Emma's arms hung over the fence that surrounded one of the arenas at Post Time Farm.

It had been far too long since she had been to her all-time favorite horse show grounds. So many memories were intertwined with her working student days here. It felt like yesterday that she arrived here for the first time where she soaked up the magic and electricity of this place.

It was the beginning of the pre-season shows, and Emma was excited to watch some of the horses she knew compete. A boarder at Live Oaks Farm was competing today, as well as one of the horses she knew from Twin Oaks. Visiting the show grounds today felt like the perfect excuse to get away from the farm – and the tension between her and Michael.

For the last several days, they had managed to at least find a rhythm when they were around each other during the day. They engaged in small talk around Sam, for his sake, but didn't make much eye contact. The tension between them may not be gone, but at least they were pretending it didn't exist when they were forced to be around each other.

Emma told Sam and Michael she would be going to the show grounds for the rest of the day after she had fed the horses this morning. Sam had tossed her an all-knowing look after telling him. They may be hiding their tension for his sake, but he wasn't stupid; he knew they were only pretending to be friendly.

Michael had offered a half-hearted "have fun" before proceeding with his morning chores. Emma had rolled her eyes as she walked away, frustrated that this is what they had become.

How was it possible they had exchanged a life-altering, passionate kiss only weeks ago? It seemed like only a dream now.

Emma returned her focus to Moose, one of the Live Oaks boarders, and his owner who were entering the equitation ring. The big bay Warmblood seemed to float over the sandy arena as he trotted along. He looked like he was born for equitation. His owner asked for the canter as they approached the first fence. Moose popped over it without much effort. Emma shook her head in disbelief; he really seemed to turn it on in the show ring versus at home.

"Did I miss much?" Emma heard a voice say behind her.

"Hey Lily! No, he just started on course," Emma replied to her friend.

Lily rested her chin on the top of the fence, her arms hanging over the post below it. The two young women watched in silence as Moose floated around the rest of the course.

They whooped and hollered when the pair completed their round and headed towards the gate.

"Lisa, you guys looked fabulous," Emma said to Moose's owner when they stepped out of the ring.

"Thank you! He has been so happy at your farm, and thanks for working him for me last week while I was out of town on that business trip. I don't think we would have done as well if he had been unworked before today!" Lisa replied, smiling down at her horse.

"Anytime," Emma replied, smiling warmly up at them. It felt nice to be a part of the horse show scene again. And it felt even nicer to get her thoughts off of Michael for once.

Lisa walked Moose back towards the show barns and Emma turned toward Lily.

"Want to go watch some of the jumpers in the Grand Prix ring with me?"

"Definitely," Lily replied, and they began walking in the direction of the Grand Prix ring.

"I'm really glad you were able to join me today," Emma said quietly, shooting a somber glance at Lily.

"Of course. How are you holding up? Have things been any better between you two?" Lily replied. Emma had called Lily in tears the day following the conversation with Michael. Since then, she had barely spoken to Lily or her other friends about it. Mostly because there was not much more to update them with, but also because talking about it felt like a punch in the gut. Emma supposed she should have expected Lily to want to know how she was handling all of this when they planned to meet up today.

"We pretend to be civil around the barn, for Sam and the boarders' sake, but Lily, I swear it's like he hates me now!" Emma bit her lip, fighting back tears that were threatening to well up. She had zero interest in crying in the middle of the horse show grounds. Emma took a deep breath, trying to calm herself.

"He can't possibly hate you, Em. He is crazy about you!"

"*Was* crazy about me. I hurt him, and I am not sure he will ever forgive me for that," Emma said.

Lily rested her hand on Emma's shoulder, the look on her face made it clear she felt bad for Emma but didn't know what to say. What else *was* there to say?

"If we are lucky, maybe someday we can at least be friends again," Emma added.

"I'm sure you will. You were such good friends before, and that doesn't just go away," Lily replied.

Emma nodded. She almost wished she had never kissed Michael. Even as she thought it, it sent a pang of hurt through her heart. The kiss had been magical, as had every single one they shared after that. Still, had they not kissed, they would still be friends and not, well, whatever they were now.

"Try not to think about it while we are here, ok?" Lily said, as if reading her mind. Surely Lily could see it written all over her face.

"I'll try," Emma said with a half-hearted smile at Lily.

They were approaching the grand looking arena now. Emma's gaze drifted to the tent where they held the VIP area during the Grand Prix. The last time they had been in that tent, Cathy had offered her this job, Liam was her boyfriend, and Michael would be hours away from kissing her. My, what a life changing night that had been.

Emma and Lily decided to sit next to the warm-up ring for a while. It was something Emma had made a habit of back in her working student days. She remembered sitting for hours in between classes watching the horses and riders warming up over enormous jumps, taking notes in her mind about how these professional riders handled each fence. Sometimes, Emma almost thought she preferred watching the warm-up ring.

A strange sound caught Emma's attention. Someone was yelling in the barn area that sat behind the Grand Prix ring. What were they saying? She couldn't make it out.

"*Probably a loose horse,*" she thought.

The yelling was louder now, and it sounded like whoever it was had to be getting closer. Oddly, it didn't sound like she was saying loose horse. It was a horse's name she was screaming.

"Loki!" a woman's voice echoed across the horse show grounds. Her voice sounded distressed and hoarse. Emma still wondered why she wasn't yelling loose horse, if he was loose, which she assumed he was.

Emma sighed as she got up. Maybe the person was new and didn't know how things worked around here. Either way, she felt she should help the poor woman since no one else clearly was.

"I'm going to go help her," Emma said to Lily, nodding in the direction of the yelling woman.

"I'll come with," Lily said, brushing dirt and grass off her pants.

Emma and Lily followed the voice around the corner of the arena. A few other people were now gathered around the frantic woman. She was sobbing and looked visible distressed.

"Are you ok?" one person asked the woman. "Can we help?" Emma added when they reached her.

"My horse, Loki, he's just...he's gone," the woman stammered between sobs.

Emma exchanged a confused look with a stranger standing next to her.

"What does she mean gone?" she thought.

"If he got loose, someone will find him," Emma reassured her, setting a hand softly on her back that heaved with sobs.

"I've been looking for hours! No one has seen a loose horse. I've been all over these grounds searching for him!"

The woman was beside herself now. Lily saw a show grounds employee golf cart not far from where they were and jogged over to him. Emma watched as Lily recalled what the woman had told her. The man on the golf cart pulled out his walkie talkie and said something into it. He waited a moment and nodded when he heard an answer on the other line. Lily jogged back over to the growing group of people surrounding the inconsolable woman.

"The show grounds office and officials said they have not had any reports of a loose horse, but they are sending people to help search the grounds now. Emma and I will help you look for him too," Lily offered, her voice soft and kind.

It *was* strange though. Normally when a horse got loose, everyone was all over it. Within minutes a stranger usually caught the horse and identified them by their halter ID, returning them to their appropriate stall. A horse simply vanishing without anyone seeing it running around was certainly odd.

"Maybe we should check the backroads behind the show grounds?" Emma suggested. She had to wonder if the horse hadn't darted away from the grounds. Still, it was strange no one had reported seeing the horse at all even if that was the case.

The woman's sobs became worse. "You think he's on the *road*?"

Oops. That may not have been the best thing to say. Still, it was a very real possibility.

"I'm parked in the back; I can start driving the backroads!" someone offered. "I can too!" someone else offered. The woman choked out a description of her horse, showing a picture of him on her phone as well.

It wasn't long before the group that had surrounded her dispersed, all on a mission to find the missing horse. One of the show officials invited her onto the golf cart so they could let her know right away if he heard anything over his radio about the horse being found.

Emma and Lily headed to the part of the property that was mostly open fields with some lightly wooded areas. She figured it was possible the horse had managed to slip back there and was either grazing or stuck in the brush. If she had learned anything from Jimmie John's great escape, it was that horses do silly things when they are freaked out.

Still, the nagging feeling remained in the back of Emma's mind. How had no one seen him running around?

"Loki!" Lily called out next to her as they peered into the patches of trees and brush. They looked into the paddocks where horses could be turned out, making sure none of those horse's tags matched Loki's. Lily's theory was he jumped into a paddock with the other horses and was hiding in plain sight. Emma had agreed, that was extremely possible.

"How long have we been looking?" Emma asked Lily as they walked back into the main area of the horse show. It was mid-day now, and the sun and humidity were at their peak. Emma slumped against a large oak tree, taking a long drink of her water. Lily sat down beside her and looked at her watch.

"Almost two hours," Lily replied, tossing Emma a concerned look.

"Maybe they found him already and we just didn't hear about it yet. We haven't seen any of the show ground officials for half an hour now," Emma replied.

Lily nodded. "Let's check in with someone, see if he was found."

The two young women stood up and walked towards the horse show office to get an update. The woman who lost her horse was sitting on one of the golf carts right out front of the office. Several people were standing nearby, and several horse show ground officials were gathered a little way away discussing something.

It took one look at the horse owner and those around her to answer their question; no one had found Loki yet. The poor woman whose horse was missing looked awful. Emma couldn't say she blamed her though. If it was her horse missing, she would look equally terrible.

Emma saw a person that had been standing near the woman when they first approached her. Emma recalled she was one of the ones that had offered to drive the backroads looking for the horse.

"I assume you didn't have any luck either?" Emma asked the older woman. The woman smiled somberly at her, clearly recognizing her from earlier. "Unfortunately, no. I drove for over an hour and so did my friend," she said, motioning to the other woman beside her who had also volunteered to drive the back roads looking for the horse.

A sinking feeling started in Emma's stomach. This was very bad.

"We searched all over the backside of the property for hours and didn't have any luck either," Lily chimed in, frowning.

"What are the show officials saying?" Emma asked in a hushed tone.

"They think at this point that he may have been stolen. He was last night's winner in one of the classes in the Grand Prix ring, so they said that's a little too coincidental."

Stolen? Emma's heart hammered in her chest. That *definitely* was not good. Emma was no expert on horse thieves, but she did know many of the horses that are stolen never ended up coming home. She hoped that that wasn't the case here.

"Have they called the police?" Emma replied to the older woman who seemed to know a lot more about what was going on than anyone else did.

"Yes, just a few minutes ago actually. They are on their way."

Emma felt sick thinking about what the poor horse owner was going through. The group of horse show officials walked back over to the small group of bystanders.

"Thank you all for taking time out of your day to help look for the missing horse. Unfortunately, there is not much else we can do except pass this issue over to the police," one of the officials said.

No one looked happy to hear this news. People began slowly dissipating, some offering a kind word to the woman whose horse remained missing.

Emma and Lily walked somberly back towards where they had parked their cars. It had certainly not been the type of day at the horse show she had expected. Sure, she hadn't thought about Michael in hours, but it wasn't for a good reason. They hadn't said much by the time they reached where Lily had parked her car.

"I hope they find her horse soon," Lily said, a sadness still in her voice.

"Me too," Emma replied softly.

"If any of the guys at Three Phases Farm hear anything, I'll let you know. They know a lot of the other grooms that have horses competing here; if anyone is going to hear any updates, it's them," Lily said with a half-smile.

"Thanks Lil, drive safe," Emma replied.

Emma headed down the line of cars where hers was parked a little farther away. She hated they couldn't help that poor woman find her horse, and that he was still out there lost somewhere. Or worse yet, stolen.

The thought sent a shiver down her spine.

They could only hope the police found whoever did this sooner than later.

"That's it Emma, just post nice and slow," Bree Lawson, Live Oaks' new trainer, called out from the other side of the arena. Emma slowed her posting like she was being instructed, and the young horse underneath her slowed down.

Emma circled, and the young horse maintained a steady rhythm.

"Lovely, just like that!" Bree said.

Emma brought the young horse down to a walk and gave her a big pat on the neck. This was one of the young Warmbloods they had just purchased, and she was becoming one of Emma's favorites to ride. Her gaits were just lovely, and other than some normal baby horse things, she was a joy to ride.

"Still no name for her yet?" Bree asked as they walked past where she was standing. Emma blushed.

"No, I still haven't come up with names for her or the other colt she came with," Emma replied. She knew she needed to think of names eventually, but her mind hadn't really been in the right place to do so yet. Emma hated the idea of panic picking a name these poor horses would have to live with for the rest of their lives.

"Well, I guess we'll just keep calling her "dark bay filly" until then," Bree said with a wink.

"I'll try and think of a name this week," Emma said biting her lip, a little embarrassed. It normally wouldn't have taken her this long to come up with a name.

"I'm headed out, but good work today!" Bree said, gathering her water bottle and phone from the mounting block where she had laid them earlier.

"Thank you and see you tomorrow!" Emma replied, turning around in the saddle.

Bree waved as she headed out of the arena towards her parked car.

Emma walked the bay filly out of the arena and onto the grass. The little filly perked her ears up; she loved walking out in the pastures. Emma smiled down at the young horse.

After they had looped the pasture a couple times, she made her way back toward the barns. Sliding off the horse's side, she led her back into the barn to untack and hose her off.

Michael was sweeping the aisleway, and Sam appeared to have just left. Michael looked up briefly, his eyes meeting hers for a few seconds before he returned to sweeping.

"That's new," she thought.

He had avoided eye contact since that awkward conversation almost two weeks ago now. Emma pulled the saddle off the filly, trying to not get her hopes up. Maybe he looked up thinking she was Bree? Either way, she didn't want to overthink it. If she was lucky, maybe this simply meant he had crossed over from hating her to tolerating her presence.

Emma set the saddle down in the tack room and sighed. It had been a long, exhausting week. The last thing she needed was to dwell on what Michael glancing her way meant. She walked back into the barn aisle but as she began to unclip the cross-ties where the bay filly stood, she felt her pocket vibrate.

Emma pulled her phone from her pocket and saw Lily's name on the screen.

"Hey Lil, what's up?"

Emma stood there a moment as Lily spoke. "Gee, and he just heard all this today?"

Emma paused, waiting for Lily to reply on the other line.

"Wow. Ok, well thanks for the update. I'll talk to you soon."

Emma hung up the phone and shook her head in disbelief. She finished unclipping the cross-ties as she led the filly outside to the wash stall.

"Everything ok?" Michael's voice said behind her. Emma turned around, eyes wide in surprise.

"I overheard your conversation with Lily, sorry. It just didn't sound good," Michael added quickly, but he didn't drop his gaze like he normally would by now.

Emma turned away from his searing, green eyes. Looking into them too long made her think things she couldn't think about Michael anymore. The worst part was the coldness in them that had been there for so many weeks now was gone. Maybe he was just that curious, or maybe he simply didn't hate her anymore. Even if he didn't hate her, he certainly didn't feel about her the way she still felt about him.

"A horse was stolen from the horse show grounds last week," Emma said as casually as she could, her back still turned as she cold-hosed the filly.

"Stolen?" he asked curiously.

"Yeah, Lily and I were there the day he went missing. We helped look for him, because at first, we all just thought he got loose, but the police are officially calling it a case of horse thief now," Emma replied.

Emma was spraying the back side of the filly, and when she turned around, Michael was standing directly in front of her, leaning against the wooden post.

"How does Lily know about the police saying the horse was stolen? What else did she say?" Michael pressed, his gaze intensifying. He seemed genuinely interested now.

Did he suddenly get better looking? Or did Emma simply forget because she had made every effort not to look at him since he had rejected her? Her heart began beating faster.

She took in a slow breath before she could answer his question.

"Some of the grooms at Three Phases, Hank and Don, know a lot of the grooms who are frequently at those show grounds. Grooms talk, and that's what one of the grooms said who works for the woman whose horse was stolen," Emma replied, dropping her eyes that had been locked into his so she could breathe again.

It had been a long time since he had looked at her like this.

"He's only interested in what happened, not you," she reminded herself.

Michael shook his head in disbelief. "Did they hear anything else?"

"Well, apparently there is now another horse missing. This time, right off someone's farm. The police are starting to see a pattern though. Apparently only horses who are recent winners of a big class are being taken within a few days of the win. The grooms are saying the horse show officials are getting nervous that this is going to affect this year's turnout for the big winter show season," Emma said, not looking into his eyes this time. Last time was almost too much to bear.

Emma felt Michael's eyes on her, and she looked up again, despite herself. She froze, fighting the urge to wrap her arms around his neck and beg him to forgive her. *That* would be big mistake.

"I can't believe there is someone taking people's horses right under their noses!" Michael replied.

"Me either," Emma replied almost at a whisper, getting caught up in the moment.

They just stared at each other for what felt like a long time. Maybe it had only been seconds, but to Emma, time stood still. That flutter of hope she had been suppressing was bubbling up.

"Lily had to get on another horse and couldn't talk long, but she promised she would keep me updated, so...," Emma trailed off. She wasn't even sure why she was telling him this. He hadn't asked. Honestly, she just wanted to drag out this moment. She was hoping the more time that passed with them looking at each other like this, that it would somehow help erase the tension between them.

"Let me know if she finds anything else out," Michael replied, sounding casual.

"I will," Emma replied.

Michael half smiled at her, then began turning around.

"Do you want to help me name some horses?" Emma blurted out before she could stop her own mouth. Why had she said that? It was clearly her subconscious grasping for any reason to continue talking to Michael.

He slowly turned back around, looking a little surprised, understandably.

"What?" Michael asked, sounding confused. Of course he was confused, what she said only made sense in her own mind.

"The new horses...the two Warmbloods. They, uh, need names," she stammered awkwardly. "I can't seem to name them, and I could use a little help. If you want."

Emma's cheeks felt red hot. This was getting embarrassing. She wasn't sure how much she cared anymore though. It's not like he could hate her any more than he already did, right?

Michael paused, processing what she had just said. He thought a moment, opening his mouth then closing it again like he wasn't sure what to say.

Oh no, she had made him uncomfortable. Maybe she should just tell him sorry, and to forget she had even said anything...

"Sure," he finally replied with a shrug, interrupting her thoughts.

Emma stood there staring at him. Did he just say sure?

"Great!" she replied, probably too enthusiastically than what the situation warranted. Emma turned her attention back toward the filly in front of her, and more importantly, away from Michael for a minute.

Emma ran her hand over the filly's velvety soft nose.

"I don't know why, but I feel like a name that starts with an L feels right," she said.

Emma could almost feel the heat coming off Michael's body as he stepped closer to her. He reached out and ran his hand down the horse's neck, looking her over.

"Lola?" he suggested.

"Kind of reminds me of Lily," Emma said, looking over briefly at him. He nodded, looking back at the horse as his face scrunched up in thought.

"You know, her coat color reminds me so much of my first horse. Maybe that's why I keep coming back to L names," Emma said softly, her fingers touched the underside of the horse's jaw.

Emma hadn't noticed, mostly because she was trying to keep her mind from the fact his body was inches from hers, but his hand was now on the side of the filly's face. Her fingers accidentally made contact with his hand, and she felt electricity flow through her. Her eyes instinctively widened and met his. He was already looking at her and she pulled her hand away quickly, dropping her gaze.

"Sorry," she murmured.

"It's ok," he whispered back.

A few seconds ticked by and neither of them spoke.

"Your first horse, his name was Lexington, right?" Michael asked, his voice still soft and low.

"Yes," she replied quietly.

"What about Lexie?" Michael suggested.

Lexie? Emma's eyes scanned the young horse's face. It fit her perfectly.

"I love it," Emma replied.

She couldn't help herself; she was looking back up at his ball cap-covered face again. Emma scanned his expression, hoping to understand what he was feeling towards her now. He hadn't pulled away when she had touched him, and he wasn't looking away now. Why?

Emma looked back over at the horse as she unclipped her and began leading her back into the barn towards her stall. She needed a moment to get her mind to stop spinning.

Michael followed her back into the barn and walked over the stall of the other unnamed Warmblood. The colt walked over to the front of his stall and Michael scratched his neck.

"What name would you like, buddy?" Michael cooed to the young horse. The chestnut colt rubbed his head against Michael's hand, enjoying the affection. Emma approached Michael and the colt, reminding herself to keep her distance. She wasn't sure how much her heart could take of being in such close proximity to Michael again, knowing her feelings were unrequited.

"You should name him too. You picked a pretty perfect name for the filly," Emma said, standing a few feet from him, and leaning against the side of the stall next to him.

"One of my favorite horses growing up at my grandpa's farm was a sorrel name Cisco. What do you think of that name?" Michael asked, turning towards her. His eyes sparkled now, lit up with the excitement of the name he had just presented her with. It was a look she had missed, had dreamed about. And now it was right here in front of her. Only, it had nothing to do with her anymore. Still, she couldn't help smiling warmly at him and his excitement.

"Michael, I love it," Emma replied. It was a cute name anyway but paired with Michael's childhood memories, it was a winner.

"Cisco," Michael said, scratching the colt's neck again, smiling broadly. It was the kind of smile that lit up his entire face.

"I think he likes it too," Emma said with a laugh, as the colt nudged Michael in the chest. Michael laughed too, the deep, genuine kind she had come to love.

Emma felt the tightness in her chest return when she thought about how she had messed all of this up. This moment was like some sort of flashback to how they once were.

Michael turned back toward her again, the sparkle in his green eyes still there. "That was fun, thanks for asking me to help name them."

He seemed to mean it.

"Hey, you did all the work, I was just here for moral support," Emma replied, holding her hands up while a grin spread across her face. It was hard not to smile when it felt they were the old Michael and Emma again, even if it was just for one, fleeting moment.

Michael gave Cisco one last pat before stepping back from the stall.

"I'm going to head upstairs. Have a good night, Emma," Michael said, looking right at her still.

"Have a good night, Michael," Emma said, her eyes locked into his.

He offered her a quick smile before he turned to head out of the barn.

She stood there watching him walk away before heading out of the barn herself.

Emma was sure she would pay for this little moment they had later, but right now, she didn't care. She was living in the bliss of it.

Chapter Five

It seemed like every time Emma spoke to someone she knew in Ocala, the words "stolen horse" seemed to come up.

Did you hear about the stolen horses? Has anyone heard if they were found yet? The questions were always the same.

It made sense, of course, since two horses in two weeks had gone missing. It seemed like all of the Ocala equestrian world was holding their breath, waiting to see if the missing horses would turn up. Or, worse yet, if anyone had heard about more horses going missing.

Word spread fast about the people who had been at Post Time Farm the day the first horse had been reported missing. Those people were now getting a lot of questions they didn't have any answers to. Emma and Lily were both finding themselves at the forefront of those conversations anywhere they went.

Just yesterday, Emma had gone down the road to the tack shop only to be cornered by a mutual acquaintance about that fateful day.

"You've had run ins with criminals, right? Do you think you could help find my friend's horse?" the mutual acquaintance had asked her.

Emma had been speechless. How did so many people know about the Bo and Clint situations? It just went to show how small the horse world was, especially in this town. Everyone seemed to know everything about everyone else.

Emma wondered just how much people knew about the situation with her, Liam, and Michael the night of the Grand Opening party. Given the guest list, it had probably spread through the town like wildfire. Emma hadn't considered it before, but she now felt a little self-conscious when she ran into people out in public.

Now though, the only thing anyone could talk about was the horses being stolen right under everyone's noses.

Emma wondered how many of the people at this eventing trial knew her secrets. Emma tried to remind herself she was no longer the hottest topic these days, even if she was at one point.

Emma checked her watch; it was almost time to head to the stadium ring to watch Clara and Cujo's round. She was glad they still had a couple hours before she needed to tack up Valentine and head to the cross country course for their final phase of the day so she could watch her friend on course.

Cujo was an incredibly talented eventing horse, and Clara was one of the bravest riders she knew. Watching them would be a treat for sure. Clara had recently moved up to the preliminary level, although Cujo had competed through advanced level with his owner. Since Cujo was getting close to twenty, his owner had let Clara, his working student, take him on and compete him. Emma's jaw had dropped a little when she saw the height of the jumps set up for Clara's round when she had gone over to do the course walk.

Emma set down her saddle that was now freshly cleaned and oiled. Valentine munched lazily on the hay in her stall. Emma smiled; her horse was like an old pro at even the larger shows now.

Emma walked up the hill towards the stadium jumping arena. Michael was probably already up there by now. He had gone to get some food half an hour ago and mentioned he would probably just go straight to the ring afterwards. He wanted to support Clara and Cujo too, which Emma thought was sweet. Of course, he was at this event because it was his job, but he certainly wasn't forced to watch her rounds or Clara's, which he had been doing all day.

As predicted, the moment between her and Michael the day they named the young Warmbloods had wreaked havoc on her mind and dreams.

In the days between then and now, Emma had hoped maybe they would take another step forward in becoming friends again, at minimum. While she was pleasantly surprised at the diminished tension between them, Michael still remained all business when they were around each other.

That was better than nothing, she guessed.

The impressive oxer was the first thing she saw after reaching the top of the hill. The announcer's voice echoed nearby, stating the name of the first horse and rider on course. Emma felt her heart racing when she thought about her own impending phase that would be here before she knew it. The stadium and dressage rounds had both gone fairly well, but the heavy rainstorm last night meant the cross country course was bound to be sloppy.

Emma paused at the side of the arena as the horse and rider on course galloped down the six stride line towards the oxer directly in front of her. The horse's ears were pricked, his attention fully on the massive fence in front of him. She watched as his muscles bunched underneath of him, powering him over the jump without exerting nearly as much effort as she thought he would need. Horse athletes, especially at the higher levels, never ceased to amaze her.

It was a shame Lily wasn't able to get away from work today to come watch as well. Emma, Clara, and Lily had been slowly becoming good friends and had been doing things together often lately. She was sure once Lily moved her horse, Annie, over to Live Oaks Farm that it would only bring them closer. Especially with all her guy drama lately, horse-loving girl friends were a bright spot in her life.

Emma continued walking down the dirt horse path that led to the warm-up arena. Before she reached it, she could already hear people calling out jumps. She smiled to herself, soaking up the horse show energy the warm-up ring radiated.

As much as she loved competing, it was nice to watch others ride and just enjoy the atmosphere for a little while.

Emma approached the warm-up ring and hung her arms over the fence, her eyes following a stunning dapple gray as it cantered towards one of the warm-up verticals. The warm-up ring was bustling, as is typical at the beginning of the phase. Horses stood around the entrance of the ring, waiting for their turn to jump around. Dark brown, wet sand slung up behind the horses as they sloshed through the sloppy arena footing. The monsoon of a rainstorm last night had taken its toll on the warm-up ring as well as the cross country courses today.

Emma was glad Clara and Cujo had already finished their cross country phase earlier in the day.

Cujo powered down the long side of the warm-up ring and Clara sat in a light two point, clearly trying to find a nice on-course rhythm while weaving around the other riders in the busy ring.

"Oxer!" Clara called out, turning toward the biggest warm-up jump there. Emma guessed she had been warming up a little while now.

Cujo had such a goofy personality in the barn, but it was funny how different he looked out here. He was all business and locked onto the fence the moment Clara began turning him in its direction.

He took a deep spot, but he tucked his legs neatly underneath himself and cleared it with a little room to spare. They landed, and Clara turned him on his haunches the other way, calling out the same jump again as they took it off the other lead.

Emma remembered her first eventing trial, and how she had almost jumped a jump the wrong direction. Most of the local schooling show jumping shows she had done back home in Ohio didn't have any limitations on which direction you could jump a fence.

"Red on the right," Emma had whispered to herself over and over, afraid nerves and the busy warm-up ring would somehow make her forget which direction she could jump it. It seemed funny how far she had already come from the schooling shows back home or even from her first big show in Florida.

Clara pulled Cujo up to a walk patting his sweaty neck as his nostrils flared. It was still humid and muggy out, probably because they were due for even more rain later this evening. Clara spotted Emma at the fence line and waved. Emma waved back and watched as Clara continued walking, doing her best to stay out of the other riders' way.

"Hey Emma," a familiar voice said behind her. Emma's heart fluttered as she turned around to see Michael standing only a foot away from her. His arm brushed against hers as he leaned over the fence, his eyes locked on the horse in front of them that cantered by.

"Hey," Emma replied, wondering why her voice sounded all cracked and squeaky. It was still hard to be in close proximity to him and not think about everything they had once shared.

"How's Cujo looking today?" Michael said casually. How was it so easy for him to act like nothing had ever happened? It was becoming frustrating.

"He looks amazing, although, the arenas are pretty sloppy. I had a hard enough time keeping Valentine from slipping during our stadium round, and we were only doing novice height. I can't imagine jumping fences like *that* when it's this slick out there," Emma replied, motioning to the biggest warm up fence as she spoke.

"Clara's a good rider, I'm sure she's got this," Michael said, shooting her a warm, reassuring smile. Her heart hammered in her chest again when he looked at her. She sighed inwardly. She was going to have to get over her feelings for Michael at some point. Emma swallowed and sucked in air before she spoke, calming herself.

"She is an incredible rider. I'm sure you're right," Emma replied.

Emma turned her attention back toward the horses still cantering around and taking jumps. Clara was still walking, and she assumed she was probably going to head up to the in-gate soon.

"How many horses until Clara and Cujo go?" Michael asked, as if reading her mind.

"Not many, I don't think. Want to head up and watch some of the other riders on course before it's her turn? I wouldn't mind getting a feel for her course again before she goes," Emma said. It was something she liked doing even if she wasn't the one riding. It made it more fun to watch, in her opinion.

"Sure," Michael replied, pushing off the fence lightly as he stepped away from it. His muscles tensed as he did, and Emma tore her eyes away as quickly as she could. No use dwelling on the way those same arms felt around her waist not so long ago.

They walked side by side towards the small metal bleachers that sat next to the in-gate. The announcer's voice rang out in front of them as another rider left the course with time faults and a few rails down. Emma was sure the sloppy ring wasn't doing anyone any favors. It looked twice as bad as it had been when she rode on it just this morning.

"Poor Clara," she thought.

Emma slid onto the first row of the bleachers and Michael sat about a foot away beside her. Out of the corner of her eye, Emma saw Clara and Cujo walking towards the in-gate. Clara seemed very sure of herself, not looking nearly as nervous as Emma was sure she would be if she was the one in the saddle about to tackle these intimidating looking jumps. Although Clara and Cujo had a strong bond and a long history of competing together. Perhaps a few years from now she would be exactly where Clara was, feeling just as confident in her own horse's abilities and partnership.

That, or Clara had an excellent poker face.

Clara gently wrapped her legs around Cujo's barrel as she asked him to walk forward toward the entry gate that was now open. Another wave of nerves washed over Emma; she was still nervous *for* Clara for some reason.

Clara trotted into the ring and halted Cujo in front of what looked like the "scariest" jump in the ring. He eyed it, and she turned him around, waiting those few long seconds before the buzzer sounded, alerting them that they could start their course.

Emma's heart fluttered when the buzzer sounded, and Clara picked up a soft canter. Emma watched as Clara began asking for more power as they approached the first fence, a vertical. Cujo's hooves left the ground as he soared over it. His confidence and business-like manner in the show ring was obvious. Emma let out a breath she had been holding after they landed off the first fence.

Clara sat in the saddle lightly and collected him as they rolled back to an oxer, soaring over it with ease. They cantered on, taking the six-stride line she had watched the dapple grey jump a little while ago. Cujo continued cruising around the course, and Emma relaxed a little more. They were still going clear, which not many riders today were pulling off.

Cujo cantered towards the oxer Clara had let him look at. Emma wondered if he was typically spooky about certain types of jumps; he never seemed to act spooky at all at home.

Cujo side-eyed the jump, and Emma caught her breath when she saw his hind leg slip underneath him briefly. Clara's expression reflected the brief, scary moment happening only strides away before takeoff. Cujo found his footing again, and jumped the oxer, although his front hoof lightly brushed against the top rail, knocking it down.

Emma groaned reflexively as it hit the ground. Cujo and Clara jumped the last few remaining fences, managing to keep them up. Emma stood up and cheered as they landed off the final fence. The announcer stated their jumping faults but that they had no time faults.

Clara gave Cujo a big pat as they exited the arena, and Emma walked up to them once they came to a halt.

"It's getting pretty slick out there," Clara said, shooting Emma a concerned look. Emma could tell she was a little disappointed about the rail they had taken down on course.

"I saw Cujo slip a little, but it looks like he recovered pretty fast," Emma replied, trying to cheer Clara up a bit.

"You have your cross country phase in a little over an hour, right?" Clara sked Emma, peeking at her watch as she spoke.

"Yes, I'm going to head back to the barns and tack up soon," Emma asked.

"Be careful out there. The ground was pretty soggy earlier, and I'm sure after being galloped on all day it's going to be pretty rough by the time you head out on course," Clara warned.

Clara's warning sent a shiver down Emma's spine. Valentine was a very sure-footed mare; she would just have to trust her horse and hope for the best. Emma just hoped she could keep Valentine at a steady pace instead of the blistering one her horse preferred. Galloping around too fast on that footing was dangerous.

"I will," Emma agreed solemnly.

"I'm going to walk Cujo out so I can get him put up before your cross country run. I'll see you in a bit!" Clara said as she asked Cujo to walk forward.

"See you!" Emma replied.

Michael had been standing a few feet away near the in-gate as he watched another horse go around the course. He turned around and waved at Clara as she began walking away and then turned to Emma.

"Do you need any help getting ready?" Michael asked politely.

"I'm ok, thank you though. Are you coming down to the cross country course to watch?" Emma asked. It seemed odd to ask, but things were different now, and it was getting late in the day.

"Of course, Em, I'll be there," Michael said, a little surprised by her question.

"Ok, I'll see you out there then," Emma said, a shy smile pulled at her lips.

Emma turned away from Michael quickly and headed back down the path to the barns.

Was she ever going to get over him? At this rate, she wasn't sure.

Emma rode Valentine at a walk down the grassy path that led across the horse show grounds. At least, that's what she was asking for, but a walk is what she was getting every other stride in between jigging.

The cross country course was on the opposite side of the grounds, which Emma thought was kind of perfect for when they would need to walk out on the way back to the show stables. However, it was proving to be a challenge as they headed towards the course. They had passed several rings already where there was jumping, and Valentine had been jigging ever since. Emma swore this horse knew she was on her way to her favorite phase, and simply walking there was not good enough.

"Don't you want to conserve your energy?" Emma said, laughing and sighing almost simultaneously as she spoke to the mare. Valentine's ears swiveled back to listen briefly, but quickly pricked towards the now visible cross country warm-up area.

As they got closer, Emma saw just how tore up the ground had become before and after the warm-up cross country jumps. She cringed; this was going to be interesting.

Emma allowed her horse to trot the rest of the way, mainly because she didn't want to pick a fight. But mostly because she was tired of trying to sit the half-walk half-trot gait Valentine had offered for the last mile. Valentine plodded along, happy to be moving forward. Emma had strapped a pair of bell boots onto her mare's hooves in hopes she would make it off this course with both front shoes intact. Although, she didn't high hopes for that considering the soggy ground conditions and the fact that Valentine was due for a shoe reset in just four days. A not-so-promising combination for leaving with two out of two shoes.

Emma saw Clara and Michael sitting in lawn chairs on the edge of the course. Bridging her reins a moment, she waved and smiled at the as she continued to trot along. There was no sense trying to stop and say hi; Valentine was in full throttle pre-jumping mode now.

Emma asked Valentine for the canter, focusing on keeping her balanced and at the steadiest pace she could. Valentine fought her, wanting to open up her canter, but Emma remained as calm and quiet as she could in the saddle. A few laps later, her horse managed to find a rhythm they both agreed to.

"With mares, it's all about finesse and compromise," Emma reminded herself.

A couple riders headed to the start box, leaving the warm-up jumps open for the moment. Emma figured she may as well see what she was up against while it was less chaotic. She didn't have much time left until she needed to be at the start box herself anyway since finding their rhythm today had taken a little extra time.

Valentine locked in on the table jump the moment Emma turned her towards it. Emma kept herself deep in the saddle, doing everything in her power to balance her horse before the jump. Valentine soared over it, shaking her head when she landed. The sloppy ground didn't seem to faze her one bit.

They headed toward the start box after a quick walk break. Emma found this helped her horse reset a little before going out on course. Valentine waited impatiently as the two riders before them went out on course. Emma circled, murmuring to the mare like always, doing her best to keep her focus.

"You have ten seconds," the woman next to the start box stated. Emma was almost a pro at timing just how big of a circle she needed to make in order to walk Valentine into the start box right when they needed to. Today, her timing was impeccable.

"Three...Two...," the woman said, looking down at the stopwatch. Valentine's front legs crossed over the threshold of the start box the moment she said, "two."

"...One...Have a great ride!"

Like a well-oiled machine, Emma asked and Valentine responded within a split second. Valentine's canter was forward and open, and Emma allowed it until they were six strides out. No use in getting in an argument with the mare this early in the course.

She was able to balance her horse and slow her down before the first jump, which Valentine took flawlessly out of stride.

The normal soft thudding of hooves on the grass was replaced today by a wet, suctioning sound as they galloped up a hill towards the next jump. This one was what looked like stairsteps, and Emma cringed when the area where horses had been taking off close to the jump came into view. It was straight mud. The jump wasn't exceptionally wide, so Emma made the executive decision to allow her horse to take a nice long spot to it and avoid the mud in hopes of keeping her shoes for as much of the course as she could. Valentine eagerly left the ground early, sailing over the steps and landing with plenty of room on the other side. Emma smiled; she was lucky to have such a brave mare.

They galloped on, the ground getting worse with each stride as they headed down the hill into the lowest part of the course. Two house-shaped tables sat in what was practically a ravine. Emma made the decision to take a long spot again and avoid the even worse footing in front of the combination. Valentine landed off the first jump and took a short stride before launching over the second jump in the combination.

"Halfway there, girl!" Emma said breathlessly as they galloped on. They took the next few jumps at a nice, normal distance since they were at the top of a hill now, where the footing was much better compared to the low points. Emma leaned slightly to the side, seeing the light grey metal on both hooves come into view when Valentine's legs were extended.

"We still have both shoes!" Emma thought, impressed they had stayed on this long. Maybe taking a bit of a long spot on the low points on course was paying off after all.

Emma slowed Valentine before the water complex, which wasn't hard since her horse still hesitated a little bit before getting in the water. Valentine splashed in at the trot but picked up her canter back on the other side. They only had three fences left.

Emma sat back, balancing Valentine as they headed into another low point on the course. She could see the finish flags now; they were almost there.

Valentine galloped towards the round top jump in front of them, ears pricked. Emma asked Valentine for another long spot, but felt her horse hesitate for half a second, which was strange for this mare. Emma heard a clinking sound in the same half-second that her horse's hooves began leaving the ground.

But something didn't feel quite right as they left the ground this time. Emma felt her horse's back leg slide a little as it tried to gain traction on the saturated ground. This fence in particular was exceptionally muddy around the base, and the half second her horse had paused had put them right in the thick of the mud.

It was in that moment that everything seemed to begin moving oddly slow, like someone was pushing a slow motion button on her brain. Emma felt the vibration of a thudding horse hoof making contact with the wood jump before she heard it. But that's where things started to go from bad to worse.

Emma was unseated, and at first, she didn't know why. It was a half second later she realized the thudding sound she heard wasn't simply her horses hoof cracking against the jump.

Emma instinctively closed her eyes, and if she didn't know any better, she would have thought she was on the top part of a roller coaster loop. She was up-side-down somehow, in mid-air.

Emma's eyes flew open as two seconds that felt like a hundred ticked by. She wasn't even sure at this point where her horse was. Was she upside down too? Or was it just her? Emma was still airborne with the ground quickly approaching, and that was all she could see from this point of view.

The hard, unforgiving ground collided with her body, making everything go black instantly. A slight ringing in her ears was all she heard. Was she awake? Emma wasn't even sure.

Her eyes opened again. How long had she been laying on the ground? She closed her eyes again for half a second, trying to listen for the sound of hooves on the ground. Or anything. Why couldn't she hear anything?

Emma took a slow breath in then out, opening her eyes again. Someone was yelling now, but they sounded so far away. She hadn't been that far from the finish flags, had she?

"Valentine!" her mind screamed. Emma tried to turn her head, but a sharp pain stopped her.

"Val...en..." her mouth was moving she thought, but the word didn't seem to want to come out all the way.

"Valentine," she croaked out this time.

Emma never really like the feeling of being drunk. She liked drinking one or two glasses of something, enjoying that light, happy buzz, and then being done. She never liked that feeling of being completely out of control of her own body. Plus, of course, being hungover was the absolute worst.

But it this moment, Emma felt like she had just chugged a bottle of vodka. Her vision blurred as she stared up at the cloudy sky, trying to make out where one cloud ended and another began. It was like she was in a foggy bubble, in a world separated from the real one.

"Valentine," she croaked again. This time, she was able to turn her head a little more. Blinking, she tried seeing through her blurred vision. Blades of grass were all she could see.

"Emma?" someone said from far away. But were they far away?

"Is she ok?!" a man's voice said, sounding distorted. But even in her foggy state, she knew that voice: Michael.

Emma slowly turned her head, looking straight up again. Someone was definitely standing over her.

"Michael?" she managed to spit out, her words coming out slow and slurred.

"We've got her," a stranger said. He was somewhere to her left side though, and she wasn't sure she had the strength to turn her head again.

"Take good care of her," Michael's still distant sounding voice said.

His face was suddenly very close. Was her depth perception going now too? His face was practically centimeters from hers. How hard did she hit her head anyway?

Emma felt Michael's lips softly brush against hers briefly, and then his face was nowhere to be seen. Was she dreaming? Had she passed out? If Michael was kissing her, she was definitely dreaming.

Seconds later, she felt something wrap around her neck, and she suddenly couldn't turn her head. The last thing she remembered after that was her body being moved from the cool, wet grass onto a stiff board.

Then, her world went black again.

Chapter Six

Emma slowly opened her eyes.

The fluorescent lights above her seemed brighter than they should be. Her head pounded, and at first, she considered closing them again. But she momentarily realized she had no idea where she was or exactly what happened. And more importantly, where was her horse?

"*Valentine,*" she thought. Her heart began to race as panic set in. She never got a good look at her. Did she go down too?

Emma cleared her throat, which felt dry. She blinked, trying to get her eyes to focus on objects in the room. None of them looked familiar, and she could hear the faint beeping of a machine. After a couple more seconds, Emma realized she was in a hospital bed.

"Emma?" a worried voice said. Michael's voice.

A brief memory flashed across her mind. Had Michael kissed her? That wouldn't make any sense. She *had* to have dreamed it. Or maybe she had been so concussed she didn't know what was real and what wasn't.

"Valentine," she managed to croak out, trying to sit up now as her memory slowly started to churn over the events of...wait, when did all this happen?

"Whoa, hey, you need take it easy. You have a concussion," Michael warned, placing a hand on her shoulder so she couldn't move as easily.

"Is Valentine ok?" Her words were coming out a little easier now, although they still sounded a little funny to her.

"She's fine, lay back and I promise I will fill you in on everything," Michael said softly, his hand still on her shoulder.

Emma leaned back against the hospital bed like he instructed, but her eyes bore into his until he spoke again.

"You and Valentine had a rotational fall over one of the jumps. You fell off and landed pretty hard on your head and neck. You have a concussion, but the doctor said you got lucky otherwise. It could have been much worse," Michael said.

"Is she hurt?" Emma said, barely hearing what he was saying about her own injuries. She needed to know how her horse was.

"Valentine fell when she landed but got right back up. She was a few feet from you trying to eat grass within minutes and seemed otherwise ok. They said she lost a shoe right before the jump and it looks like she slipped which caused her to fall over the jump," Michael said as reassuringly as he could.

Emma started to try and sit up again, but Michael placed a hand back on her shoulder and gave her a look. Emma opened her mouth to speak but Michael beat her to it.

"I already called the vet; he's looking at her right now. But the vet at the show said she will probably just be a little sore from the fall and will obviously need to see the farrier. Otherwise, she's totally fine, Em," Michael said, as if reading her mind.

"We should probably pack that foot until the farrier can come out. She may be sore from it coming off and…," Michael held his had up, stopping her rambling and chuckling a little.

"Emma, we have it handled. Clara took her home and already packed her foot. She's in good hands, I promise. Try to focus on resting, ok?" Michael said, his eyebrow raised in concern.

"Look who's awake," the doctor said as he entered the room.

Michael walked over and shook the doctor's hand.

"Well Miss Walker, it looks like you had quite the fall today! You were very lucky. Nothing is broken, and other than taking it slow and getting lots of rest for a while, you can recover at home. I've had the nurse begin your discharge paperwork," he said, smiling warmly over at her.

"How long until I can work with the horses again? Or ride?" Emma asked nervously. How was she supposed to do her job under these conditions?

"It's hard to say right now as we will need to monitor your recovery. Everyone heals at their own pace. Brain injuries are serious, so be sure to take things slow, ok? But I'm sure you'll be back to normal soon," the doctor replied.

Emma didn't like that answer but tried to focus on the positive. No broken bones, which would have meant a longer recovery, and most importantly to her, Valentine was ok.

Emma took a deep breath, letting it out slowly.

"Thank you," she said to the doctor before he left the room.

Michael shot her a concerned look. "You *are* going to rest like the doctor said, aren't you?"

Emma gave Michael a playful smirk.

"I'll try," she replied.

"Emma...,"

"I'm joking Michael. Yes, I promise to take it easy until I'm better," Emma replied, rolling her eyes at him but smiling anyway.

"Good. I'm going to hold you to that," Michael said, looking serious.

He was still looking at her, his expression concerned.

Everything was so fuzzy after she fell. It was hard to make out what really happened. She swore she had felt Michael's lips on hers. But if she said something and it was all a weird, concussion-induced dream, that would make things really awkward again. The last thing she wanted was to take a step back in becoming whatever they were now. Friends, at the very least, it seemed.

And right now, Emma was enjoying the way he was looking at her; like he truly cared.

"I'm just going to feed her a treat and say hi, Michael. I'll be fine," Emma said, shooting Michael a look that said she was perfectly capable of walking to the barn to pet her own horse.

It wasn't as if she was going to black out because she so much as left the house.

Besides, she had been resting for three full days straight, and she was going a little stir crazy. She missed her horse and the way the barn smelled and pretty much everything that didn't involve sitting in bed or on the couch.

"Fine, but I'm escorting you out there to make sure you don't pull any funny business," Michael teased.

"It's not like I'm going to hop on bareback and go galloping across the field, Michael," Emma said, rolling her eyes.

Michael looped an arm through hers. "Sure, you won't," he teased back. She pretended to be slightly annoyed that he wasn't letting her walk to the barn without being assisted, but the way his strong arm felt against her skin made it hard to say no. His touch still sent electricity through her.

Emma had been surprised, given how awkward their relationship had been prior to her fall, how attentive Michael had been since. Emma was released from the hospital the same day, luckily, but Michael had insisted on sleeping on the couch in the house in case she needed him. She had tried offering him the guest room, but he refused stating he was comfortable on the coach.

One night had turned into three, and now here they were, the morning of day four and he was still acting like she was a fragile, porcelain doll. Although, she had to admit, all the attention felt nice.

The only problem with Michael fussing over her in her concussed state was that his attentiveness had a shelf life. Emma was trying not to get used to the way he looked at her with concern or insisted on being by her side whenever he wasn't working. Because as soon as she was back to normal, so was their relationship.

Emma still didn't know if Michael had actually kissed her while she was lying there half-blacked out on the cross country course, but she still hadn't had the nerve to ask and ruin whatever time she had left of him acting this way.

Cathy had called every day to check in on her, and Michael had also been filling Cathy in regularly since the day of the fall. Michael made it clear to Cathy that he was making sure Emma was resting and doing all the boring things the doctor instructed. It was really the only reason Cathy hadn't cancelled her vacation with friends to come up and take care of Emma herself. Now, it seemed Michael and Cathy were practically best buds. It was a little strange to Emma at first, but she was glad there wasn't any animosity between them because of what happened between him and Liam.

The barn doors were already open as they approached, and the smell of horses and hay wafted from the barn, all but hitting her in the face. She drew in a long, slow breath, enjoying it while she could before she had to return to her isolation inside.

Valentine's low, friendly nicker melted her heart.

Emma pulled her arm free of Michael's and reached out to touch her mare's velvety nose as she approached. Emma gently rested her forehead against Valentine's. She was beyond grateful her horse hadn't been seriously injured during their fall.

The farrier had said Valentine's hoof was a little bruised since she stepped on her shoe while it was half off, but Clara had been packing it with something that she said seemed to be helping. The vet also offered some pain medication for a little while since he said Valentine may be sore from where she hit the ground.

Overall, the two of them had been extremely lucky.

"I'm so sorry," Emma coed to the mare.

"You know you couldn't have done anything differently," Michael said quietly, placing a hand on her shoulder.

"I know, I just hate that she was in any pain at all," Emma replied, never taking her eyes off her horse.

"If it makes you feel better, I think you had the most injuries between the two of you," Michael said, chuckling.

"Actually, it does," Emma said, briefly looking at him with a half-smirk.

"Emma!" Sam's cheerful voice echoed down the aisle.

"Hey, Sam," Emma said, smiling his way as he approached.

"Michael says you have been trying to sneak out here for days," Sam said, winking.

"He has practically put padlocks on the doors," Emma replied, tossing Michael a devious look.

"Don't worry Miss Emma, we have everything handled out here until you're completely healed. Bree has been working the horses, and Michael and I have been making sure the barn is up to your standards. Oh, and Clara has been taking special care of Valentine when she comes out to ride Cujo," Sam said.

"Thank you for keeping things running smoothly while I'm on house arrest," Emma teased.

"Don't worry, you'll be back out here and riding again in no time," Sam replied, giving her a sympathetic look. He seemed to sense how much it was killing her being away from the barn and the horses.

Bree walked in the barn leading young Rosey behind her.

"Emma, how are you feeling?" Bree asked as she approached.

"Much better, thank you. How are the new youngsters doing?" Emma asked, glancing at Rosey.

"They are all coming along very nicely, especially this one. She is something special," Bree said, patting Rosey's dark, sweaty neck.

"Yes, she is," Emma agreed.

Emma hoped it wouldn't be too much longer before she was allowed to ride again. Missing these early training days with the young horses she loved like her own was almost unbearable.

"Alright Em, you should probably head back inside," Michael said, his green eyes showing concern under his ball cap.

Emma sighed audibly and planted a kiss on Valentine's nose.

"Fine, I will head back to solitude. It was nice seeing you guys," Emma said, glancing from Bree to Sam.

"Feel better!" Sam called down the aisleway as they headed back towards the house.

Michael walked back with Emma. When he opened the door to the house, Emma walked straight over to the couch. She slumped into it, grabbed the remote, and pulled the throw blanket over her legs.

"I know, I know, I should take it easy the rest of the day," Emma said sarcastically.

Michael walked across the room and sat next to Emma on the couch. His eyes met hers, a serious look on his face. Michael gently took her hand, and Emma tried to remind herself to keep her emotions in check.

"Do you know how scared I was when I saw you lying on the ground like that?"

"I'm ok though, Michael, really," Emma reminded him.

"I know that now. But then...," he trailed off, shaking his head. "Em, there was a moment I didn't know if I had lost you," Michael said almost at a whisper.

Emma suddenly understood why Michael was being so over-protective of her. If she had seen his seemingly life-less body on the ground, how would she react? Especially considering he had lost his late fiancé.

Before her fall, they were barely even friends. He had been so hurt and so angry. Could it be possible that this life-or-death situation had somehow pushed those negative emotions from his mind?

Emma didn't dare hope this shift in this way he treated her was permanent. When she was fully recovered, Emma was sure he would slowly forget the incident. Would he go back to being angry with her? Or remember how she had hurt him by running off to consider Liam's proposal?

Maybe, at the very least, this meant they could truly be friends again.

Emma had waited for this moment for the last several weeks. The doctor had finally cleared her to return to normal work during yesterday evening's appointment, and that included riding. Her heart practically sang when the words "ok to ride" had come out of his mouth. Emma ran through the list of every horse she wanted to work the following day. Of course, he had cautioned her not to overdo it. Figures.

Still, she was excited to be allowed to do *any* riding. The last week she had been able to sit and watch Bree work the horses, and the last few days she'd helped turn out horses, (although Michael kept deliberately grabbing the spicy ones before she could), and feed grain.

But now, it was a new day, and the reality was beginning to sink in that she hadn't ridden in what felt like forever. She was bound to be sore, at minimum. Emma tried to remember the last time she had gone this long without riding. She had not had a serious riding injury take her out like this one had. She had been one of the lucky few people, let alone horse people, she knew who hadn't broken any bones.

Nerves fluttered in her stomach as she pulled on her rubber boots. Why was she nervous? Surely muscle memory would kick in and take over the moment she swung her leg over that first horse's back.

Emma closed her eyes a moment as she walked towards the barn. The sun felt warm on her face, and she could feel the shift in temperature lately as they moved further into fall. The humidity as of late hadn't been quite so ruthless, making for some perfect riding days that she had been missing out on.

Michael and Sam turned around when they heard her footfalls on the barn's aisleway floor.

"She's back!" Sam greeted her with a warm smile and an arm around her shoulders.

"It's good to *be* back!" Emma replied.

Michael smiled warmly at her and gave her arm a gentle, affectionate squeeze. "See? I told you that you would be back out and riding before you knew it."

Truth be told, the weeks between the fall and today had felt endless, but she wasn't about to complain about that now. After all, she was still walking on eggshells, waiting for the other shoe to drop between her and Michael.

Michael had slept on the couch for a full week before finally making his way back to his own bed in the barn apartment. Even then, he came over most evenings after work to sit with her and watch movies. He claimed he was trying to make sure she followed doctor's orders, but he didn't seem to be all that miserable spending time with her either.

Emma found herself becoming too comfortable with their frequent hang outs. The way they laughed and talked, she all but forgot about the fact they had been estranged not so long ago.

As the weeks continued on, his visits to the house became less frequent. She felt him pulling away a little more each day, as she had expected him to. But there was something strange about the way he looked at her now. It wasn't like he had when he was angry with her, but it also wasn't like after they shared the kiss the night of the storm.

Emma still couldn't place it. She could only hope whatever forced bonding they did the last couple weeks was enough to repair what she had broken.

"Who are you riding first?" Sam asked, pulling her from her thoughts.

"Um...I was thinking maybe I should get on my own horse first. I know her best, and it might be a nice warm up before riding the green ones," Emma replied.

"I'm sure Valentine will like that," Michael added.

Emma turned toward her horse and slid the halter over her head, leading her to the grooming bay. The nerves she felt earlier came flooding back. What was wrong with her? She *wanted* to ride!

Emma brushed off the feeling and focused on tacking up her horse instead. She groomed her slowly, enjoying the feeling of the soft brush flicking dust off her mare's smooth coat. She felt her worry slip away with each stroke.

Emma slid the saddle onto Valentine's back, then the bridle over her ears. She walked slowly towards the mounting block, forcing the tension and fear from her body.

Swinging her right leg over the saddle, she settled into her seat and clucked her mare on at the walk. It felt so natural to be back in the saddle. Why was she so concerned in the first place?

Emma took her time warming up at the walk and trot, enjoying every second of it. For her, riding was like breathing. Like second nature. A piece of her had been missing and felt so off when she had been forced to stay away from the horses for so long.

Emma asked for the canter, and Valentine stepped into her usual, smooth, rocking horse style gait. The rest of the world faded away as she felt the connection between her and her horse. She hoped there would never be anything else that would force her away from being in the saddle again.

Emma brought her horse back down to the walk, patting her neck.

"That was fun, huh? Let's end there today, Val," Emma said, a wide grin spreading across her face.

She saw Michael leaning against the wall of the barn aisle, just inside where it was shadowed. His arms were crossed against his chest, and he had a look on his face she couldn't quite read. What was he thinking? Maybe he was making sure she didn't panic and fall off again or something.

A pang of sadness ripped through her heart when she considered the fact that while she was finally healthy enough to ride, that meant she was ok enough to not be checked on all the time by Michael. Was this the end of their movie nights and him pretending to be friends?

Emma slid from her mare's side after walking her out. Michael had disappeared back into the barn minutes after she had seen him standing there. She tried not to think about him as she cold-hosed her horse, and instead thought about the next horse she wanted to ride. Bree had been raving about how well Rosey was doing, how she was a total natural over jumps. From the rides she had watched earlier that week, Emma had to agree.

"That's who I will ride next," she thought. Feeling the mare's progress in the saddle herself would surely be exciting.

Emma pulled the young Thoroughbred from her stall and tacked her up quickly in her excitement.

"Good choice," a voice said warmly behind her.

Emma turned to see Bree walking down the aisle.

"Hey Bree! I know, I can't wait to see how much improvement she has made since the last time I rode her."

Emma and Bree chatted about the mare's progress as Emma slid the bit into the horse's mouth.

Emma mounted up and walked the mare forward. Gingerly asking for the trot, she felt the mare softly upshift, a dramatic change from how she used to blast into the trot before.

"Bree has clearly been putting some work into this one," she thought.

Emma trotted figure eights, doing a few trot to walk to trot transitions. She asked for the canter now, and a smile tugged at her lips as she felt the mare go into a soft, balanced canter. Rosey cantered rhythmically around the arena, practically floating along. She had come so far in such a short time. Bree was spot on; this mare was something special.

Emma saw Bree sitting on the mounting block, watching her ride. She brought Rosey back to a walk, patting her neck.

"Bree, she is absolutely lovely. You've been doing an amazing job with her!" Emma said, shaking her head and smiling brightly.

"Rosey is a quick learner! You should see her over small fences; she is a little rock star. Why don't you take her over the little cross-rail over there and see for yourself?" Bree suggested, pointing to the jump at the other end of the arena.

"Sure!" Emma replied, turning the mare away from Bree and picking up the trot. Emma found a nice balance and rhythm, keeping the mare in front of her leg as they trotted down the long side of the arena.

Rosey's ears pricked forward as she locked onto the cross-rail, now about seven strides away. Emma felt that same nervousness from earlier in the pit of her stomach as they moved closer to the jump. Seriously, was she nervous about a tiny cross-rail? Bree had made it clear Rosey was a very point and shoot ride over jumps.

Four strides out. Now three.

Emma felt her muscles tense. Then, it was like the real world suddenly faded out from in front of her. It was as if someone had pushed the slow motion button in her head again. The world went black, and in her mind, she was flying through the air and landing on the hard, unforgiving ground of the cross country course again. The flashback seemed to take control of her consciousness, and suddenly, fear was the only emotion running through her mind.

Emma gasped and found herself pulling on the reins and the mare swerved away from the jump at the last minute in confusion. Tears welled in Emma's eyes as she jumped from Rosey's back. Bree ran over to her, taking the reins from Emma.

"Are you ok?" Bree asked, a look of concern on her face.

Emma shot one quick, apologetic look at Bree before running full speed away from the arena. She didn't stop running until she was safely in the house with the door closed behind her. Tears poured from her eyes as sobs rattled her body. She slid into the nearest dining room table chair, burying her face into her hands.

She had been terrified to jump even the smallest cross-rail. But it wasn't just the paralyzing fear before the fence that had her so rattled; it was the fact that if she couldn't move past this fear, everything she had worked for would be down the drain. If she couldn't find the courage to jump again, where did that leave her? Training young horses was a very large part of her job.

Emma couldn't *not* jump them. They were in training, and they needed to be worked consistently. Bree couldn't do it all by herself.

Sobs rocked her again as Emma considered the fact the fall had affected more than just her body.

It had destroyed her mind.

A light knock on her front door made Emma jump. She hit pause on the romantic comedy movie she had been watching.

She had been hiding out in her house since she had her panic attack while riding Rosey that afternoon. Emma was mortified at how she had reacted, leaving Bree standing there holding Rosey's reins as she fled. Looking back, it was a cowardly move. She didn't even know what had come over her. The fear had taken hold of her mind and it somehow triggered some innate flight response. Still, she should have explained to Bree what had happened and owned up to it.

But her own reaction to approaching the jump had scared her, and worse yet, made her question if she would be able to jump ever again. The thought of losing everything and crying about it right there in front of Bree was the last straw before she found herself running away.

Emma checked her watch; Bree was probably wrapping up for the day right about now. She wondered if it was her knocking on the door. It might not be such a bad thing if it was as Emma owed her an apology at the very least.

Emma opened the door to see Michael standing there in front of her. Concern was obvious on his face and the space between his eyes was scrunched up.

"Can I come in?" he asked softly.

Emma nodded, opening the door wider so he could walk through. She felt a tightness in her throat and swallowed hard. She did not want to cry again, especially in front of Michael.

Emma sat down at the kitchen table and Michael followed suit. He reached his hand across the table and wrapped it around hers. His green eyes locked onto hers from under his worn baseball cap. Emma felt her heart race as his hand brushed against her skin. Her eyes flitted from his hand on hers to his eyes that were still locked on her face. He tilted his head slightly, as if to read her expression better from beneath his ball cap.

Emma had promised herself she wouldn't read too much into anything Michael had done while she was injured. But she was technically better now, right? Well, clearly something was wrong with her mentally, so she should be writing this off as a pity touch. At least, that's what she was telling herself to keep from doing something stupid: like kissing him.

"Em, what happened today," Michael's soft voice and piercing green eyes asked her.

Emma bit her lip, taking a moment to gather her thoughts. She had been asking herself that same question all day.

"I was fine riding on the flat, but as soon as we approached that jump...," her voice broke, and Emma took in a slow breath to steady her emotions. "Michael, it was like I was right back on that cross country course. I could all but see myself catapulting through the air, and the blackness as I hit the ground," Emma winced reflexively as she spoke.

"Emma, you went through something pretty traumatic. That's not just going to magically disappear right away, no matter how much you want it to," Michael said, squeezing her hand. It sent electricity through her, making her heart skip a beat. She hated that his touch had this effect on her still.

"But...what if I can't move past it? Riding is my whole life," Emma replied, her voice breaking again.

"Time heals everything. I promise you, it does. There was a point in my life I thought I would never get over Jane or even be able to drive down the road where she had her car accident. I was even afraid to drive myself for weeks knowing what happened to her. But one day you will wake up and that memory won't consume you like it does now," Michael said. His hand ran up her arm and then landed gently on her face. He seemed to catch himself and pulled it back reflexively.

Her heart hammered in her chest. Why had he done that? And why did he seem to pull back so quickly, almost like he hadn't meant to touch her that way?

Michael cleared his throat and shifted in his chair. "Just take it slow, you'll be fine in time," he said, offering her a warm smile. His hand hadn't returned to hers though, and for some reason it bothered her.

"Looks like it was a pity touch after all," she thought.

Emma forced herself to focus on the conversation and not Michael's reaction to touching her.

"I'm sure you're right. I'll talk to Bree tomorrow and let her know I need to just ride who I can on the flat for a little while. Maybe another few weeks or so in the saddle will build my confidence back up to the point where I can try jumping again," Emma said, trying to sound positive. Although, she was still a little worried the fall would hang over her head forever.

"Good idea," Michael said. He suddenly stood up, making it clear he was about to head out. It looked like their days of movie nights and hanging out were definitely over. Emma hated that she had been right about those days having a shelf life.

"Have a good night, Emma," Michael added. He turned and started walking towards the front door.

Suddenly Emma felt the desperate need to say something, anything, to make him to stay a little longer. She missed him, and their forced bonding during her concussion recovery had only intensified her feelings for him. Emma was learning pretty quickly just how awful unrequited feelings were.

Emma was no stranger to word vomit. It had been the ruin of Cathy's Grand Opening party. But sometimes, it just felt like her mouth was briefly disconnected from her mind and attached to her heart. And what the heart wants to say is usually not what the mind would agree to.

"Why did you kiss me?" Emma blurted out as Michael's hand began turning the doorknob.

Michael froze for what felt like several minutes, but it was probably only ten seconds. He slowly turned around, the shock lingering in his gaze.

"What?" he mumbled, looking confused.

Oops. She had really done it this time. Oh well, what could it hurt at this point? For days he had been pulling away, so it wasn't like there was much to ruin anymore. Well, except maybe whatever thread of friendship they had rebuilt. Too late for that now.

"When I fell. You...kissed me...didn't you?" Emma stammered.

Emma quickly tried to focus her mind on that awful day. Had she just talked like a crazy person about something that hadn't even happened? It had all been such a blur. Still, it felt *so* real. Why was he still staring at her, mouth slightly agape? Oh gosh, maybe she had dreamed the whole thing after all...

"I...I didn't know you knew about that," Michael stammered, shifting his weight. He still looked surprised. Surely he hadn't expected her to say *that* weeks after her fall.

To be fair, she had been basically unconscious. Clearly not unconscious enough though, since she had been right the whole time. He *had* kissed her. Emma felt her heartbeat pick up as the realization that she hadn't made the kiss up after all. So, that begged the question; *why* had he kissed her?

"I wasn't completely convinced it wasn't a dream this whole time, to be honest," Emma said, her cheeks flushing red now.

Michael blinked, tilting his head to get a better look at her.

"Why didn't you say something before now?" he asked.

"Honestly, I doubted it really happened and I didn't want to ruin...," Emma slammed her mouth shut, realizing she had begun saying something she didn't mean to. Again.

"Ruin what?" Michael asked, taking a step towards her now.

"Ruin the way you...you know what, forget I said anything," Emma said dismissively. This was a can of worms she did not want to open. What was she supposed to say? Hey, I liked how it felt pretending we were together and that you didn't hate me anymore, but I know it's only because you thought I almost died. Honestly, it's probably why he kissed her on that cross country course anyway.

"Emma," Michael said softly, almost empathetically, taking a few more steps toward her. He was a mere foot away now. Emma tried to control her breathing, but his close proximity was not helping.

He placed one hand on her upper arm. "Ruin what?" he repeated. Her face had surely given her away, and he wasn't dropping it. She sighed audibly. There was nothing else to do but let the chips fall where they may.

"Michael, I liked the way things were after I had my concussion. I know it was probably all out of pity. But when we watched movies, laughed, and talked. Well, it just felt like how it did before...," Emma trailed off. No use saying out loud what had driven them apart in the first place. Her own selfish mistake. A regret she couldn't take back no matter how much she wished she could.

"I was worried about you," Michael said, barely above a whisper.

"I know, but see, that's just it. You only were around me because you felt sorry for me, or you wanted to make sure I wasn't going to re-injure myself, am I right?" Emma fought the urge to roll her eyes and let out a sigh. Why had she opened her big mouth? This conversation was getting more awkward by the minute. She may as well kiss what was left of their friendship goodbye.

Michael stood there, staring at her, speechless. Could she blame him? Finally, he sighed heavily, and his shoulders relaxed.

"I'll be honest, I kissed you because I was terrified that I could lose you right then and there. I didn't really think about it, I just sort of...," he paused, then shrugged, "I just did it."

"Do you regret it?" Emma replied, her eyes dropping to the floor after the words came out.

Michael paused and seemed to think about her question.

"No," he replied.

Emma wondered what that meant. Did he still had feelings for her? Or he didn't regret it because he thought she was on death's door? Probably the latter.

"Are you still angry with me, then?" Emma said sheepishly.

"I wasn't angry for long, Em. But what you did after everything that happened between us, after telling you how I felt about you...well, it hurt me. And I don't think I'm over that just yet."

"So it's possible you will forgive me?" Emma asked, searching his face desperately for answers.

"I do forgive...," Michael began.

"You know what I mean," Emma said, cutting him off. Who cares about being forgiven if the feelings Michael had for her never returned and she was left forever regretting what could have been?

"I don't know, Emma," Michael said, shaking his head.

Tears welled in her eyes. She had hurt him, that much she had already guessed. But quite how badly she hurt him, she hadn't known the extent of until now. His hurt was justified though; he had literally confessed his feelings to her when they were searching for Mandy. She had kissed him on the night of the storm and they had kissed again at the campsite. And then, she left without a word to consider a proposal to another man. From his perspective, his reservations toward her made sense. That didn't mean it didn't break her heart any less, though.

Michael finally dropped his gaze. He seemed to feel guilty about the tears still threatening to spill from her eyes.

"Have a good night, Emma," Michael said softly as he turned and headed out the front door.

Emma stood there, processing their conversation.

If ignorance is bliss, she had just shattered whatever was left of hers. Finding out the kiss had been real had not made her feel the way she wanted it to.

In fact, Emma felt even worse than she had before. Michael's words swam around her mind.

What if this was it for them?

Emma sank into the nearest chair and let her mind replay the last night they had spent hanging out together. Memories may be all she had left of them now.

Chapter Seven

Emma dumped a full wheelbarrow of fresh sawdust into an empty stall. Setting it down, she checked her phone.

"Be there in five!" a text from Lily read.

Emma smiled to herself. This was a day she had been excited for all week. Actually, longer than that. She had thought about it since Cathy bought the farm in the first place.

Lily was finally moving her mare, Annie, to Live Oaks Farm. Emma couldn't be happier about the timing of having her best friend be around the barn all the time. With only a little over a month to go before starting veterinary college, Lily was soon going to be only a part-time employee at Three Phrases Farm. This meant she wasn't getting the free board benefit she had as a working student or full-time employee.

It's funny how time flies. It seemed like not so long ago she and Lily were back in Ohio talking around a bonfire about her future working student position and starting veterinary school. But here they were a year later, and nothing was the same as it was back then.

Emma's awkward conversation with Michael about him kissing her had backfired, as expected. Michael may not be avoiding her like when she first arrived back from her trip with Mandy, but the semblance of friendship they had rebuilt while she was recovering from her concussion was on shaky ground. Emma still wondered if he would ever be able to get past what she had done and the hurt that caused him.

"Is Lily almost here with Annie?"

Michael's voice made her jump. His eyes darted from the phone in her hand to her eyes. Emma felt her face flush pink knowing she had been thinking about him while he had walked in behind her.

"Yes, she is a few minutes away," Emma tried to keep her voice even.

"Good, I'm sure you're excited to have her here," Michael said, smiling warmly at her.

Small talk? Well, at least they were back to that.

Emma offered the warmest smile she could manage in return. She hoped it conveyed everything she wasn't saying.

"Emma, I think your friend is here," Sam said, interrupting them. Both Emma and Michael's heads turned toward Sam's voice. He was peering around the corner of the exterior of the barn.

The rumble of a trailer and sharp whinny coming from the mare inside confirmed it. Emma headed out of the barn towards the now parked trailer. A familiar face slid from the driver's seat of the truck pulling the trailer.

"Hank!" Emma said, rushing over to her previous Three Phases Farm co-worker.

"Miss Emma! How is life at your new farm?" Hank asked, his eyes scanning the breathtaking farm in front of him.

"It's everything I hoped it would be," Emma said wistfully. Truly, running this farm was what her younger self's dreams were made of.

"Hey, Em!" Lily said as she appeared from the other side of the truck.

"I'm so happy you're here! Clara has been talking all week about how excited she is about our adult saddle club," Emma said to Lily with a wink. "Clara said to tell you welcome, and she's sorry she couldn't be here. The barn she works at is at a competition today."

"Clara's not the only one who is excited! There is no way I'm surviving working and vet school without you guys," Lily replied, concern written all over her face.

Lily was one of the smartest people Emma knew, but somehow Lily still seemed to doubt herself. Emma made a mental note to be sure she was there for Lily as much as she could be in the coming months as she transitioned into a new phase of life.

Emma followed Lily to the backside of the trailer and together they lowered the ramp on the sandy ground with a thud. Annie called out again from inside, triggering a wave of reply whinnies from inside the barn across from them.

Annie backed out of the trailer, swiveling her ears in each direction as she took in her surroundings.

"This is your new home, Annie," Lily murmured, stroking the mare's stiff neck, which was turned toward the far side of the farm. "It's hard to believe were at Three Phases Farm for a year!"

"I know, it blows my mind I've been in Florida almost a year as well," Emma said, shaking her head in disbelief.

The young women headed into the barn where whinnies and nickers echoed as they led Annie to the stall Emma had prepared that morning.

Annie found the flake of hay Emma had tossed in the corner of her stall and settled into her new home easily. Lily hung her arms over the stall's door, watching her mare casually lip at her hay.

Michael and Sam walked into the barn aisle, and Sam tipped his hat at Lily, a boyish grin on his face. He didn't say anything, so Michael chimed in. "Welcome, Lily," Michael said warmly.

"Thank you," Lily said smiling back at Michael before her eyes flitted to Sam. Sam dropped his gaze, but Emma was pretty sure she saw a smile under his cowboy hat.

"I'll help you get your tack," Michael added, heading towards the trailer out front with Sam on his heels.

Emma smirked; Sam was acting strangely around Lily. She was sure that could only mean one thing.

After Lily's tack was put away, the girls headed out to the back part of the field. Emma had promised Lily a tour of the cross country course since she hadn't seen it yet.

"How are things with Michael?" Lily asked, her voice low.

Emma grimaced briefly, giving away their less-than-ideal standing.

"So, not great then?" Lily added.

"Oh Lily, you know me, always putting my own foot in my mouth," Emma said sarcastically, rolling her eyes.

"Oh no. What happened?" Lily said, shooting Emma a worried look.

"I confronted Michael about the kiss when I was laid out on the cross country course."

"Wait, he did what?"

Oops. Boy, she was really striking out lately. Emma bit her lip, remembering she hadn't told Lily, or anyone for that matter, about the kiss the day she fell.

"Yeah, sorry Lil. It's been a rough couple of weeks. I guess I have a lot to fill you in on."

Emma told Lily everything that had gone on between her and Michael since her fall.

"And since you told him, he has been acting like it never happened?"

"Kind of. He wasn't exactly acting super weird or avoiding eye contact like he was when I came home from the trip with Mandy. But he has been not as talkative. Then this morning, he walked right up to me and started making small talk. I'm probably reading too much into it, but I'm telling you Lily, it felt different."

"Well, maybe he realized he can't be mad at you forever. I don't get why two can't just realize you're meant for each other and be together already," Lily teased, nudging Emma in the arm.

"Easy for you to say. Speaking of, how are things going with that guy you have been seeing?"

Now Lily was the one rolling her eyes.

"Chris is fine, he's nice."

"He's fine and nice?" Emma repeated, sarcasm dripping from each word. She shot Lily a look, prompting her for more information.

"I don't know, it's just not *there*, you know? That spark. I should probably just break things off with him; I'm starting vet school soon anyway. The last thing I need right now is a boyfriend."

"You sound like me when I first came to Florida, and look how that turned out," Emma said, looking over at Lily with a smirk.

"That's because Liam swept you off your feet. Then, you and Michael were apparent soulmates. With two hot guys pining after you, of course you were going to cave!" Lily teased.

"Lily!" Emma's jaw dropped a little and then she let out a deep laugh.

"What, tell me I'm wrong!"

"Well, if it makes you feel better, I rejected Liam's proposal and now Michael wants nothing to do with me."

"Psh, a temporary setback," Lily said, waving her hand in the air dismissively. Lily seemed so sure she and Michael were meant to be. Too bad he didn't see it that way.

"Ok, so back to your love life," Emma said.

"Or lack thereof," Lily sighed heavily. "Yeah, I've barely seen him anyway. I mean I'm busy, but I've been putting off seeing him for a week now because I hate break ups. Even necessary ones."

"That makes two of us," Emma replied.

The girls walked another few feet in silence, pondering their respective relationships. What was left of them, anyway.

"How is riding going since your fall?" Lily finally said, breaking the silence.

Emma shot her a look, frowning slightly. Another touchy subject.

"Yeah, I thought that may be the case," Lily replied, understanding exactly what that look meant.

"I'm fine on the flat, but when I tried jumping the tiniest cross-rail last week, I froze up and panicked. I literally jumped off Rosey and bolted back to the house with my tail between my legs right in front of Bree and Michael. It was mortifying!" Emma said.

"Remember when I fell off that crazy hot pony years go? The one Maggie got from the auction that I had first ride on?"

Emma nodded. That pony had bolted from one side of the ring to the other, broncing the entire time. Poor Lily held on until the very end, and consequently, was launched into the wall of the indoor arena. Her arm was broken during the fall, and it took months for Lily to get back on a horse again, even her own.

"I remember," Emma replied softly.

"After that, I was terrified to ride again for a long time," Lily said softly.

"How did you move past it?" Emma asked.

"When I felt ready, I waited until the barn was quiet, until no one was around. I don't know why, but somehow, it felt like less pressure. I told myself, I'm just going to get on and walk. I remember walking for almost twenty minutes, which I felt would have looked silly if anyone had been there. Then, I trotted exactly five minutes and got off. But you know what, after that, I was alright. I rode with you and Hailey the very next day. You will figure out a way to move past your fall, I promise."

Emma thought about Lily's words. Maybe she was on to something.

Emma looked out of the open barn doors at the breathtaking sunset. The clouds had hot pink streaks running through them, and the sun hung low and orange in the sky.

There were maybe forty-five minutes left of daylight. Lily had gone home a couple hours ago, Sam left for the day, and Michael was sweeping up the last of the hay on the barn aisle floor. After that, she knew Michael would head back to his apartment for the night.

Emma turned her attention back toward the bridle she was cleaning in the grooming bay, twisting it into a perfect figure eight pattern. She had cleaned all of her own tack and the tack of the horses she normally worked, and now she was merely killing time.

Emma heard the clunking sound associated with Michael putting the broom back in its place on the wooden barn wall. She considered looking up but instead pretended to be focused on the bridle she was tinkering with. Of course, she could figure eight a bridle in her sleep at this point.

Emma felt Michael's eyes on her. She refused to look up, slowly putting the thin piece of leather through the metal buckle instead.

"I think I'm going to head upstairs," Michael said, and she could still feel his gaze directed toward her.

Emma tried to act nonchalant.

"Ok," she replied, not looking up from the leather she was winding around the back half of the bridle.

"What are your plans tonight?" Michael added, after a moment of silence in between her words.

"Oh, I might get Valentine out," Emma said, trying to sound casual, her eyes only flitting up to meet his for half a second. Emma couldn't stand it; she had to know what the expression on his face was like.

"Do you want me to stick around while you ride?" he pressed, sounding slightly concerned.

Emma's hands stopped moving and her eyes met his.

"No, I'm ok," she replied quickly, her voice sounding a little edgier than she intended.

"Oh, ok." Michael's tone held surprise, like he hadn't expected that answer.

"Thanks anyway," Emma added lightly, hoping she didn't sound too rude before.

"Sure. Well, I guess I will see you in the morning," Michael said, sounding a little confused.

"Have a good night," Emma replied, looking his way briefly before returning to her work.

Michael walked out of the barn, and she could hear his boots on the stairs and then on the floor above her head.

"*Finally!*" she thought. She needed to be alone for her plan to work.

Emma all but jogged to Valentine's stall, slipping the purple halter over her head. Leading her down the aisle to the grooming bay, she clipped either side of her halter. Wasting no time now, she gently tossed the saddle pad and saddle on her back, girthed her up and slipped the bit into her mouth and the bridle over her ears. Nerves racked her as her mind strayed, thinking about what she was about to do.

Emma took in a long, slow breath, releasing the tension from her body the best she could. Transferring that negative energy to her horse when she was in the saddle wouldn't do her any favors.

This evening, there was only one thing Emma was determined to accomplish: jumping again. Lily's words had rattled around in her thoughts all day. It made perfect sense, really. Take the pressure of everyone's eyes on her away and take things at her own pace. Just knowing no one was here watching her was like a weight lifted. If she circled in front of the jump a hundred times, she wouldn't feel embarrassed. If she couldn't jump at all, no one would know, and she could try again later. If she walked around and did nothing else, no one was here to comment about it.

Emma took a deep breath, blowing the air out slowly. Valentine's ears swiveled from the open barn doors back to Emma, and Emma rested her forehead against Valentine's soft forelock.

Perhaps she should have tried jumping with her own horse in the first place. Emma wondered if it would have made a difference. Not that she didn't trust Rosey, she was a great young horse, but she wasn't Valentine.

Valentine had quite literally saved her life in more ways than one. Less than a year ago, this horse had bravely jumped a metal gate to help her escape Bo who was chasing her down with a motorcycle. She had been calm in the face of a bear, and light on her feet as they cantered through heavy brush away from Clint. There was no one and nothing in this world she trusted her life with more than this little mare. Between conquering courses and running from bad guys, Valentine always had her back.

Now, it was time for Emma to set aside her fear and trust her once more.

Emma walked the mare to the mounting block, swung her leg over and settled lightly into the saddle. She looked up, taking in what might be the prettiest sunset she had seen on Live Oaks Farm thus far. It was like the sky was displaying her favorite color, just for her.

They walked for what felt like forever, and Emma let the gentle four beat gait of Valentine's walk ease her mind as she prepared herself. She knew she needed to warm up quickly and get right down to business before she chickened out.

Emma asked her horse to trot, and the pair wound around the deep arena sand, changing directions as she asked Valentine to move off her leg. Emma smiled; it also wasn't so long ago this horse would not have responded so perfectly to her aids on the flat. Dressage had certainly done wonders for both their flat work and jumping.

Valentine broke into her floaty, rocking horse canter that was still to this day the easiest canter she had ever sat. How had she gotten so lucky with a two-hundred-and-fifty-dollar auction horse?

The pair cantered around the ring, changing directions twice, and Valentine offered two flawless lead changes. Her balance and lead changes had only gotten better since they started eventing.

This was it. Her horse was perfectly warmed up and responding to her every aid. If Emma didn't know any better, she would think Valentine knew the importance of this ride and was on her best behavior because of it.

"*Trust your horse,*" she thought.

Emma leaned over the pommel of the saddle and wrapped her arms around Valentine's neck. "I trust you," she said out loud. The mare's ears swiveled back, listening to her owner's voice.

Emma settled back into the saddle, gathering her reins. A small cross-rail was set up on the quarter line. She took in one more deep breath and asked her horse to trot out underneath of her as she blew it out. Valentine trotted along eagerly, feeling the shift in her rider's position. She was on full alert now, knowing what this change in her owner's seat meant. Valentine was already hunting the jumps, eyeing each one as they passed by until the cross-rail was directly in front of them. Her ears were pricked in its direction, the mare's pace picked up slightly. Emma felt her body relax a little more when she felt the mare lock on. Valentine wasn't afraid, and her bravery was rubbing off on Emma.

Six strides away now, Valentine balanced back, using her hind end more and picking up her pace just a little. Emma steadied her and looked over the jump to the other side. Staring at the jump wasn't going to do her any favors.

"Three...Two...," Emma though, counting strides in her head, keeping Valentine in front of her leg.

"One."

Emma closed her eyes as she felt the mare's muscles bunch underneath of her as they left the ground. Then, they were in the air. She kept them shut, remembering and enjoying the feeling of flying. Valentine had missed jumping; this much was clear by the way she was jumping this cross-rail like it was much larger than it was.

All four hooves met the sandy ground, and Emma's eyes flew open, a smile breaking over her face now. She had done it. What had she been so afraid of?

Valentine shook her head, cantering on as she looked for the next fence. Emma turned her head, spotting a small vertical a few strides away. Valentine leaped over it eagerly, and Emma was beaming now.

After landing off the vertical, she pulled Valentine back up to a walk and patted her neck affectionately.

"Thank you," Emma whispered to the mare.

Emma slid off Valentine's back and led her to the grooming bay, still smiling for ear to ear. She sponged her saddle area off since she had hardly broken a sweat, brushed her down, and fed her a handful of horse cookies.

"You earned these today," she murmured, scratching the mare's neck. Emma led Valentine back to her stall, and the mare began lipping at the half pile of hay she had left from her dinner. Emma hung her arms over the stall door, resting her chin on top of it, watching her horse eat.

Emma felt like she was on top of the world, like she could do anything. Horses seemed to have that effect on her; they made her feel strong, smart, and beautiful every time she was in the saddle. And tonight, after conquering a fear that had haunted her for the weeks following her fall, she had never felt more alive.

Emma hadn't quite felt that "I almost died" moment until right then. Maybe because she was so focused on so many other things, namely, riding and jumping again. Now, she was realizing just how lucky she really was. Michael's reaction to her fall during those early days of recovery suddenly made more sense.

She couldn't believe she hadn't realized it before given her near death experience. Life was too short, and there was no promise she would see tomorrow. As much as she loved horses and trusted them, especially Valentine, there was still risk involved.

Emma's emotions swelled, getting the best of her. Maybe it was the high of jumping again or the near-death experience suddenly making her realize just how poorly the fall could have gone. Either way, she found herself walking with purpose out the barn doors.

"This could go terribly," her inner voice reminded her. After all, it wasn't the first time she had acted impulsively with a not so ideal outcome. But there was no stopping her now. She was determined to see if the spark between her and Michael was still there for him as much as it was for her. When he kissed her in her half-conscious state on the cross country course, she had felt it then too. It's why she held onto the fact that it really had happened so tightly. Had he felt what she felt and was pushing those feelings away because of the hurt she caused him?

If this went poorly, she knew it was possible they would be doomed to barely be friends for however long it was Michael continued to work at Live Oaks Farm.

But if it didn't...

Emma tried not to get her hopes up. This was going to be a long shot. She walked up the stairs that led to Michael's apartment, feeling butterflies doing somersaults in her belly with each passing step.

"This is crazy...," she thought.

But she knew that the minute she started walking towards his apartment, didn't she?

Emma paused at his doorstep. She could hear the faint sound of a laugh track on the television just behind the closed door. Michael let out a deep laugh too. Whatever he was watching he thought was funny. Good. Maybe that meant he was in a good mood and might just forgive her impulsiveness and what she was about to do if it backfired. Which, let's face it, was a high probability.

Emma knocked softly on the door. She took a step back, leaning against the railing of the decking. Her heart hammered, and she felt the blood drain from her face, down her hands, and to her feet. What was she doing?!

Emma heard the door creak and saw it opening slowly in front of her. Michael's face behind it showed a mixture of surprise and concern. He probably assumed something was wrong. In a way, it was.

"Emma?" his tone relayed the same concern his face showed under his worn ball cap.

Emma's heart continued to hammer. She was frozen there, hands gripping the railing so hard they were turning white. Her mouth was going dry. Was it too late to run the other way?

No. She was done running. She had faced up to one fear, and now she was going to face another.

"Is everything ok?" he added when she didn't answer. Michael took a step down onto the decking area where she stood. He glanced from her out at the back of farm then back to her. She wondered what her expression looked like. Emma hoped it wasn't showing every single thing she felt. She took a quick breath in then out, and tried to muster the same courage she felt before walking up the stairs.

Taking the two steps towards Michael that closed the gap between them, she looked into his concerned, green eyes. For some time now, Emma realized she might be falling in love with Michael. Of course, she had made some poor choices along the way that kept her from realizing it sooner, but staring at him now, she was sure she was falling for him in every way possible. How could she not? Michael was the best guy she knew. And Emma hoped that he still cared for her too.

She held onto that feeling of hope that whatever he still felt for her was enough to justify what she was about to do.

Emma leaned in, her hand wrapping around Michael's neck, lightly touching the back of the ball cap he wore. She froze a moment, her lips lingering half a centimeter away from his, her eyes darting to his one last time. But to Emma's surprise, she felt his arms wrap around her waist as he pulled her closer.

Emma closed her eyes, her lips brushing lightly against his in a feather-light kiss. She leaned in closer now, placing both hands around his face. Electricity ran through her as he pressed his lips against hers, more intensely this time.

Michael pulled away gently. How long had they been kissing? It was like time was standing still. Thirty seconds? Maybe longer?How I

Her heart hammered again, this time for a totally different reason. Michael hadn't pushed her away, and what's more, he had kissed her back.

Surprise still lingered on his face, but a smile was tugging at his lips. What was he thinking?

"I didn't know if I would get another chance to do that," Emma said, barely above a whisper. She wasn't sure if he understood what she meant.

Michael nodded; his eyes were still locked on hers.

"I understand," was all he said. His fingers twisted into hers. Emma fought the urge to ask him what it all meant. This was a big step forward, and she had probably pushed her luck enough for one night.

"Have a good night, Michael," Emma said, quickly kissing him on the cheek before turning on her heels towards the top of the staircase. Emma hoped by tomorrow Michael would have time to think about tonight's kiss. When she reached the bottom of the stairs, she closed the barn doors behind her, and leaned against them briefly as she caught her breath.

Closing the barn up for the night, she couldn't stop smiling.

Because tonight, she had discovered one thing: Michael most definitely still had romantic feelings for her.

Chapter Eight

Emma had wondered if today would be different.

After all, she and Michael had kissed last night. That had to mean something, right?

"Em, are you almost ready?" Clara's voice pulled her from her thoughts. Clara and Lily both stood in front of her with their horses fully tacked up. Clara's eyes flitted from the saddle still in the trailer back to Emma. Emma's cheeks flushed pink, and she pulled the saddle from the trailer's saddle rack, placing it on top of the saddle pad already on Valentine's back.

"Coming!" Emma replied. Oops, she had been slacking. Or daydreaming, technically. Butterflies danced around inside her when she thought about last night's kiss and everything it could change.

"Hurry up!" Lily teased and Clara and Lily headed towards the plastic mounting block they had brought with them. Valentine craned her neck, watching her two horse friends walk away from her.

"Alright, Val, I'm hurrying," Emma told the mare who looked like she was seconds from whinnying at her friends who were much too far away for her liking. She pulled the leather billets through the girth's metal buckle and pulled the girth around her mare's barrel.

It was one of those perfect, almost humidity free days. Well, as humidity free as you can get in Florida, that is. Fall weather was in full swing. Back home in Ohio, Emma imagined the trees were beginning to change colors, the air cool and crisp. Here in Ocala, of course, that's not exactly what fall was like. Still, it meant the possibility of perfect riding weather days just like this one.

Lily had sent a group message to both her and Clara last night suggesting they go on a trail ride, making a joke about how the adult saddle club needed to make their trail riding debut. Lily mentioned she was feeling the pressure of beginning preparation for veterinary college beating down on her and said a trail ride would be a great way to blow off some steam. How could Emma say no? Especially since Clara was all about it.

They decided to keep the ride earlier in the day to take advantage of the best possible temperature. That meant Clara and Lily would be in the barn first thing in the morning, giving her and Michael zero time alone before they left for half the day. Of course, Sam probably would have interrupted them first thing anyway, even if Lily and Clara weren't showing up earlier than usual.

Emma would just have to be patient to see how Michael acted around her after last night's kiss. She smiled to herself as she pulled the girth tight on the other side of her mare. He had kissed her back, and that was all that mattered.

Sliding her helmet onto her head and pulling her thick hair into a ponytail, she grabbed the bridle from the trailer's tack room and headed back over to her horse. Valentine let out a sharp whinny, clearly worried her friends would go galloping off without her any minute now.

"Ok, ok, we are going lady," Emma said, chuckling a little as she slid the bridle over her mare's ears.

Emma walked Valentine over to the other two women who were mounted up and waiting on her a few feet away from the mounting block.

"Let the first official trail ride of the adult saddle club commence!" Lily stated excitedly as the girls walked towards the head of the trail.

Emma was suddenly thankful for good girl friends who loved horses as much as she did. Truly, she had been fortunate to have Lily move down here around the same time she had and to have met someone as lovely as Clara.

Clara asked Lily how shopping for her on-campus housing was going. The two chatted about what kinds of things Lily should get for her new place. Emma smiled, glad Lily and Clara had become friends as well. It seemed Lily could use all the support she could get right now. Emma couldn't even imagine going back to college for another four years. But if anyone could do it, it was Lily. For some reason, she just didn't realize quite how brilliant she actually was, based on how stressed she was about starting school.

Emma's attention turned from her chatty friends to the tropical foliage around her. No matter how many times she rode through Ocala's forests, it never ceased to take her breath away. Tall pines blowing in the light breeze lined either side of the path they were walking down. Clara and Lily had fallen silent and were both taking in the gorgeous scenery around them now too.

"So, I broke things off with that guy I was seeing," Lily said, breaking the silence. Emma and Clara's heads whipped around to look at Lily.

"Are you ok?" Emma said softly. It looked like it wouldn't be the ideal day to talk about how things were finally looking up with Michael like she had planned.

"I mean, break ups are no fun, even if you weren't in love with the guy," Lily said, rolling her eyes and scrunching up her nose. Emma couldn't agree more. Breaking up with Liam, despite not being actually in love with him, had been awful.

Clara made a groaning sound. "Ah Lil, that's awful. I'm so sorry," she said, genuine sympathy in her voice. Clara was probably the sweetest, kind-hearted person Emma knew.

"It's ok guys, I'll be fine. Sometimes you just wonder if you'll ever meet *the one*, you know?" Lily said, her gaze on the path in front of them.

"I get that!" Clara said, shaking her head.

Emma remained silent. It wasn't the time to chime in that she felt like she had already met *the one*. Clara and Lily both turned to her, as if expecting her to chime in too.

"You both are young, beautiful, and talented ladies. I'm sure you will find the right person when the time is right," Emma said.

Clara and Lily exchanged a look.

"We get it, Em, you're crazy about Michael," Clara said with a wink.

"Oh, that's kind of a sore subject for Emma still...," Lily began. To be fair, the last conversation she had with Lily about Michael had not been a positive one.

Emma bit her lip, trying to decide if she should say anything about Michael or not. Lily caught the indecision on her face though.

"Ok, spill," Lily prompted, shooting Emma a look that said she knew her well enough to know she was keeping a secret.

"Well, I jumped again last night for the first time since my fall, and right after that I walked up to Michael's apartment and kissed him," Emma said, her cheeks flushing pink.

A snort-laugh escaped Lily. "You go girl!" she said before letting out a deeper laugh.

Clara joined in and then Emma began laughing along too. It did seem a little funny looking at it from their perspectives.

"So, how did he react?" Clara asked, her eyes wide.

"He kissed me back," Emma said, grinning now. She couldn't help it. Even she couldn't believe things had turned out the way they did.

"Emma! That's amazing!" Lily replied.

"I'm not quite sure where we go from here, but it was a pretty good step in the right direction," Emma said.

"I'll say! See, I told you it was only a matter of time before you two crazy kids figured things out," Lily replied.

Emma looked over at Lily, suddenly feeling guilty.

"I'm sorry Lil, I didn't want to say anything since you are going through a breakup," Emma said.

"Em, I'm happy for you. This guy I was dating wasn't the right person for me and I knew it. You and Michael have had your fair share of ups and downs. It was about time you guys made up," Lily said with a wink.

Emma felt only half relieved. Still, she felt bad about rubbing her happiness in Lily's face right now. Even if Lily didn't seem to see it that way.

"Who's ready to stretch their horse's legs?" Lily said, pulling Emma from her thoughts. Emma looked out at the open field a few feet ahead of them. It was the perfect terrain for a nice gallop.

"My horse is always ready for galloping!" Emma replied.

"So is Cujo!" Clara chimed in.

"Race you to that live oak at the edge of the field?" Lily asked, pointing out the tree.

"You're on," Emma said, her competitive side showing in her words.

"Ready? Five, Four, Three, Two," Lily counted.

"One!" All three of them said simultaneously. Valentine, Cujo, and Annie blasted out of the forest almost neck and neck. They stayed within a stride of one another until they were halfway across the field.

Hooves pounded on the ground and Emma could barely hear Valentine's rhythmic breathing between footfalls. Annie, the ex-racehorse she was, pulled ahead. Her long legs ate up the ground with ease. Cujo was close behind, still almost keeping stride with Valentine.

Emma felt a surge of energy as Valentine suddenly launched forward, her stride opening up. Valentine's breaths came quicker as her muscle powered her forward. Emma smiled as the mare continued eating up the ground. She was neck and neck with Annie now, but Annie was beginning to pull ahead. Valentine never did like being at the back of the pack or being left behind for that matter. Now was no exception. Emma felt the mare pushing off the ground harder, her stride quickening. She was pulling just ahead of Annie now.

The tree wasn't far now, and the rest of the field was a blur behind them. The thud of hooves on the ground was the only thing Emma could hear as the three horses passed the large oak tree. Valentine had managed to come in first by a nose.

The three women pulled up their horses, and everyone was gasping for breath. They were all smiles though; what a rush that had been.

"That was fun!" Clara said, beaming.

"It sure was," Lily replied, her smile matching Clara's.

Emma was all smiles too.

It looked like today was turning out to be a great day, in more ways than one.

Emma waved as Lily's and Clara's cars headed toward the front gate of Live Oaks Farm. What a day it had been!

Their trail ride had lasted longer than she originally anticipated, since every time they found a deviation in the trail that led down a longer section of the path, they took it. After their exciting gallop through the field, they mostly walked and trotted, spending time talking. Emma had to admit, it had been exactly what she needed. Probably exactly what Lily needed too.

"Did you guys have fun?"

Emma smiled to herself, recognizing the voice before she turned around.

"We had an amazing day," Emma replied, turning around to see Michael casually leaning against the side of the barn, his arms folded across his chest, a goofy grin on his face. How long had he been there watching her stare out across the farm as her friends drove away?

Michael walked across the lawn towards her. Emma froze, her mind churning over every possibility of what he would do or say next. He seemed in good enough spirits, not like he regretted their kiss.

It was the first time she had seen him since last night. Sam had all but shoed her way from the feed room when he heard her friends were on their way over to meet up for the trail ride. Michael had been fixing a fence board one of the young horses had managed to break during night turnout, and he was busy when they had arrived back from the trail ride.

Emma tried to control her breathing as he got closer to her.

"About last night...," Michael began, but trailed off.

Emma felt her heart skip a beat. She desperately read his facial expressions, hoping to guess his next words. To her disappointment, there was nothing readable in those green eyes of his.

His fingers lightly ran up her arm, giving her goosebumps before resting on her shoulder. His eyes flitted from where his hand touched her skin back to her eyes.

"Yes?" she said, gulping. Her skin felt electrified by his touch. He was still looking at her, as if deciding his next words carefully. Each moment he didn't speak again was agonizing. *What* was he going to say about last night?

"I want to know what you were thinking," he finally said softly.

"I jumped Valentine last night," Emma replied. She figured she may as well start at the beginning. Michael tilted his head, intrigued by her answer.

"Em, that's great. I told you it would only be a matter of time," he replied.

"I wasn't so sure. But I decided to trust my horse and give it a try without anyone watching me."

Michael seemed to be putting the pieces together in his mind.

"Is that why you were acting so strangely before I went upstairs yesterday?"

"Yes, I wanted to be alone when I rode. I thought maybe if the pressure was taken off I could jump again," Emma replied.

"After that, I felt differently. I guess it took truly moving past the side effects of my fall to realize just how much worse it could have been. I was so focused on getting better to ride again, and then jump again, that I never let myself truly process that my fall could have...," Emma trailed off, shaking her head, her voice breaking.

"I know, that's how I felt when I saw you lying on the ground that day," Michael said, stepping just a little closer now.

"So, I decided life is too short, and that I wanted you to know exactly how I still felt about you," she said as her gaze dropped to the ground a moment before meeting his again.

They stood in silence, staring into each other's eyes for a moment. It was like they were having an unspoken conversation.

"Em," Michael's voice seemed hesitant, and he pulled away slightly.

Oh no, not again. Emma tried not to panic, but she didn't like the look on his face.

"I never stopped having feelings for you, even when I was hurt or angry with you. I care about you and that won't ever change. But...," he paused, seemly collecting his thoughts.

"But?" Emma chimed in, waiting impatiently for him to go on.

"But I think we should take things slow, after everything that happened. I still need some time to work through that."

Emma let out the breath she didn't know she was holding. Take things slow? That she could live with. A wide smile broke over her face.

Michael laughed. "What?" he asked, reading her expression.

Emma leaned in, tipping Michael's ball cap back, kissing him slowly, and her head began to spin. She pulled away, still smiling, a devious look on her face.

"Michael Hale, I will take things as slow as you want. As long as we are together."

Michael smiled back, leaning in and kissing her back.

"I missed you, Emma," Michael murmured, his lips still lingered on hers.

Emma knew this was only the beginning of the trust she surely needed to regain with Michael.

But in this moment, she didn't really care how long that took.

Emma hung up the phone, shaking her head.

Michael looked over his shoulder, setting down the full wheelbarrow of fresh sawdust.

"What is it?" he asked, reading the concern on her face.

"That was Lily. Hank just heard through the groom grapevine another horse was stolen from the horse show in Wellington this time. Apparently, this is the second horse in Wellington to go missing this week," Emma said gravely.

"Oh gee, another one? How many horses have been stolen now?" Michael asked, his eyebrows bunching together in concern.

"Four or five total, I think," Emma replied. Four or five too many. It made her sick to think about anyone stealing one of the Live Oaks' horses. Those poor owners. She couldn't even bring herself to imagine what that must be like.

"That's awful. Do the police have any idea who is doing this?" Michael asked.

"So far, no. The thieves have been incredibly careful, whoever they are. The police said these are definitely professional horse thieves," Emma replied.

Michael's fist clenched and then released. The thought of someone taking other people's beloved horses seemed to make his blood boil just as much as it did hers.

Emma watched his expression relax, and then shift.

"What is it?" Emma asked curiously. The twinkle in his eye made her curious.

"I have a surprise for you," Michael said, his smile reaching his eyes. "I was going to wait until later, but I figured with all the bad news this morning, maybe we needed a little good news sooner than later.

Emma tilted her head, smiling now.

"What is it?"

Michael walked over to her, his arm wrapping around the small of her back.

"I have tickets to that show jumping competition in Miami. You know, the one you've been talking about all week?"

"The one where the horses are literally jumping on the beach by the ocean?" Emma gasped, her jaw dropping a little.

"That's the one! But it gets better," Michael added, his green eyes twinkling again.

Better? What could be better than watching horses jump around Grand Prix fences literally next to the ocean?

"Guess who is competing in that Grand Prix?"

Emma thought for a moment, and suddenly her eyes went wide as she realized there was only one horse in particular he could be referring to.

"Jimmie John?!" Emma asked, gasping again.

"You got it," Michael said, seeming pleased with himself.

That competition was only a couple weeks away. Michael must have paid a pretty penny to get tickets like this so last minute. It made Emma happy to know Michael was thinking about her in future terms, even if it was only weeks from now.

"Michael, thank you," Emma said, sweetly kissing him on the cheek.

"Get a room, lovebirds," Sam teased, emerging from the stall he was cleaning behind them. Emma turned around and Sam winked at her. "Just kidding. But seriously, Em, Michael, I'm glad you two finally figured things out."

Emma shot Sam a look of appreciation.

"Thanks Sam. And don't worry, there is a special lady out there for you too!" Emma said.

Sam smiled, but there was a sadness to it. He didn't seem as convinced as Emma was.

"You're welcome," Sam replied, pushing his full wheelbarrow out of the barn towards the manure pile.

Emma made a mental note to be sure they weren't too nauseating in front of Sam in the future.

It was hard to believe a week had passed since she had kissed Michael and since she had started jumping again. In that week Emma had continued to build her confidence and jump some of the younger green horses. Rosey especially had been exciting to jump, and she was turning out to be everything Bree had said.

Lily made Emma and Clara promise to make a riding pact once a week. Emma was sure the stress of starting vet school was a factor, but Emma and Clara had agreed willingly anyway.

After all, riding with those girls was something she needed for her own sanity too.

Chapter Ten

"Thirty Seconds."

Emma nodded to the woman next to the start box holding the stopwatch and circled Valentine in front again.

Her heart hammered in her chest. This was the first time she had been out on a cross country course at an eventing trial since her fall. She knew this day would come eventually, and she had prepared herself mentally and physically for it.

Still, fear was creeping into her with each second that ticked by. Emma felt like she was barely keeping it at bay as she took a long, slow breath in and out.

Valentine jigged under her, immune to the fact that the last time they were on this very course, both of them had taken an eventful fall. To her horse, this was just another day she got to gallop and jump. Which, of course, were two of her mare's favorite things to do.

"Ten seconds."

Emma's heart skipped a beat, then raced faster.

"The ground isn't saturated this time," she reminded herself. Valentine was sure-footed, and the fact that she had lost a shoe and slid was a one off. At least, that's what she was trying to convince herself.

"Five, Four, Three...,"

Emma blew out a breath she didn't realize she had been holding as she made her final circle, pointing the mare a stride away from the start box. It felt like deja vu except this time, she hoped things would turn out much differently.

"...Two, One...Have a great ride!"

Emma swallowed hard and the reins slipped through her fingers ever so slightly, the only signal her horse needed to begin galloping in the direction of the first jump.

The pounding of hooves on hard ground began drowning out her thoughts. She focused on each footfall and the rhythm of her mare's canter. Emma let herself get lost in it as the wind whirled past her ears, making a slight howling sound.

Valentine took the first jump, a rolltop, out of stride, hunting the next jump the moment all four hooves were back on the ground. Emma had wondered if her mare would have some sort of PTSD from this place, but apparently Emma was the only one who was still shaken by the incident.

Another two jumps down, and Emma felt her muscles relax slightly as she settled into the course. She and her horse loved cross country; Emma was going to have to get past this fear. Of course, she knew when signing up for this competition that it wasn't going to be easy. She also knew it was the final step in moving on from her fall for good.

"I'll be right there waiting for you at the finish flags," Michael's words drifted into her mind. She pictured him sitting right there at the edge of the course with Lily and Clara. All of them would be cheering her on...

Emma gasped. Valentine's hoof caught on an uneven patch of ground causing her to break stride momentarily.

"Focus," she thought.

Emma sat up in the saddle, her eyes on the horizon as they made their way towards a house-looking jump in the distance.

Valentine took a deep spot to it, taking off awkwardly, mainly because Emma saw a closer distance. Luckily, the mare picked up her feet up and cleared the jump anyway. Emma thanked her lucky stars her horse was brave; Valentine easily could have refused and no one would have blamed her.

It was her own fear trying to take over again. Emma knew better; Valentine did best taking everything out of stride at a slightly longer distance. Getting in her face and getting her too backed off to the jumps never worked out well.

Emma promised herself she wouldn't overthink her distances the rest of the course. If she just let her mare roll out underneath of her and trust her distances, they might just make it through the rest of this course.

Valentine splashed through the water complex, her eyes locked on the log-type jump a stride out. It was funny how the water complex used to be the thing she feared most out on cross country.

They galloped on, and Emma let her horse open up her stride as they headed into the shaded portion of the course. They jumped two more fences, steps, and another roll top with ease this time.

It was the exact moment Emma felt comfortable on course that she saw the next jump in the distance. She felt the blood drain from her face, a chill suddenly rip through her body.

There it was, the very table that they had fallen over. Valentine's stride didn't let up as they began their approach. Of course not, to her mare this was just another jump. To Emma though, it was a jump that held a terrible memory she had hoped was long forgotten.

Staring it down now though, it felt anything but forgotten. It may be in a different location on course now, but the image of this jump had been forever burned into her brain. The thudding sound of her body hitting the hard ground, the panic as she strained to see if her horse was laying on the ground next to her with a broken leg...

Emma suddenly felt the urge to hurl. She swallowed, taking a breath through her nose and out her mouth as she fought the nausea. Her horse was fine; she was fine.

"Focus!" her mind reminded her again.

It was just another jump, just like the ten others they had already conquered so far. Emma shifted her weight back in the saddle, focusing her attention on the other side of the jump and balancing the horse under her.

Valentine would jump this like she had everything else, with enthusiasm. All she had to do was push her fear aside and get out of her mare's way.

This time, Emma didn't count strides or look for a spot. This time she was going to let her horse do what she did best and stay out of her way when she did. Trusting her horse to get her over this was her only option.

Emma sat up in a soft two point, letting her horse continue to roll out at a forward pace in front of her leg. Valentine's muscles gathered under her, and she pushed off the ground at exactly the right distance. Emma smiled, closing her eyes mid-air. They were flying, and nothing was taking them out this time.

Valentine landed, galloping away from the fence as she sought out the next one, completely unaware of the significance of the previous jump. But Emma did, and she was still grinning from ear to ear.

They crossed through the finish flags a few jumps later, and that same smile was now radiating off of her. The cheers from Michael and her friends echoed across the field like she had imagined. But the pride she felt from conquering her fear was like nothing she had ever felt before, proving to Emma, once again, that the bond she shared with her horse meant she could do anything.

Emma walked out of the barn towards the pasture in the furthest right-hand corner of Live Oaks Farm.

Just when she thought nicer, cooler weather had finally found its way to Ocala, Florida was here to remind Emma just how far south she was. A bead of sweat trickled down her forehead, threatening to run into her eyes. Again. She wiped it away, rolling her eyes.

Back home, she never in a million years would have thought the words, "is it winter yet?"

To be fair, Ohio winters and Ocala winters were vastly different. Ice, snow, and sub-zero temperatures were the only things a northern winter had to offer, none of which are conducive for riding horses. Ocala, however, had proven to be quite lovely most of the winter, with temperatures that would make northerners jealous.

But here Emma was, thinking about how winter would bring more horse shows and lovely temperatures to her now-home state. As she got closer, Emma watched as several horses pulled thick mouthfuls of grass from the ground. The live oaks, which she now knew she could never possibly get tired of looking at, blew in the light breeze. A breeze Emma had wished was a little stronger on a day as sweltering as today had turned out to be.

Emma smiled, her eyes running over each horse one by one. Their coats gleamed in the sun, and she couldn't help but think how happy they all looked. It was one of her favorite things about running this farm: lots of happy horses. Her smile quickly turned to a frown. Emma counted the horses, this time carefully.

"*No!*" she thought.

There was one horse missing: Cujo.

Emma froze, her eyes scanning the pasture once again to make sure he wasn't laying down somewhere causing her to miss him the first time. Still, no Cujo.

Emma tried to keep her mind from going to the worst-case scenario. Cujo had placed second in his division at the eventing trial the other day. Emma couldn't deny that coincidence. It was the horse thieves' MO.

She racked her brain for any possible chance a thief could have made it on property without any of them noticing. Emma had ridden several horses that morning, but there was absolutely no way she could have missed anyone walking right past the arena, which is what they would have to do in order to reach the pasture gate.

Sam was still here, and he had been in the barn most of the day. Michael had been mowing most of the afternoon, but surely he would have seen someone lurking around. Of course, she hardly expected them to pull through the front gate with a horse trailer.

Odds were they would lead the horse somewhere they could get out and then load them on the road. But where? This wasn't like when Mandy was taken. They couldn't exactly sneak a horse through the fence or toss them over.

Emma put both hands on the fence rail in front of her, steadying herself against the sudden lightheadedness that threatened to overtake her. She focused her mind on the layout of the farm, brainstorming any possible area of weakness they could get a horse through.

None came to mind; this place was completely surrounded by fencing and the only entrance was the one at the front of the property guarded by the gate that only a select few knew the entry code. Could they have somehow figured out the code? Emma didn't dare consider the option of someone close to her being involved with any of this.

Suddenly Emma was turning on her heels, running full speed towards the barn. Michael had finished mowing half an hour ago and was surely back there by now.

"Michael!" Emma screamed, but her voice was cut off by her own heavy breathing as she pushed forward across the grass. She hoped he might have heard her, but it looked like that wasn't the case. She ran harder, a panic rising up in her with each step.

"Not Cujo," she thought. Clara would be devastated.

Emma slowed before entering the barn aisle. No need to spook the horses she had brought in from the other pastures a few minutes ago.

"Mi...chael," Emma gasped for air, her hands on her knees now as she tried to suck in enough air to speak again.

Michael's eyes were wide as he peeked his head out from inside the feed room.

"Emma?" his voice leaked concern as his gaze locked on to the still-panting Emma.

"Cujo...he's not in the pasture," Emma stammered, still barely able to breath.

The concern on Michael's face increased as he walked quickly over to her, placing a hand on her back. Emma slowly stood up, her eyes locking onto Michael's. She was sure her face told him just how panicked she was beginning to feel. How was she supposed to tell Clara?

Until they had investigated further, Emma wondered if she should even tell her. Why upset her unnecessarily?

"Tell me everything you know," Michael asked, placing both hands on either side of Emma's shoulders.

"I went to the back pasture to bring in the rest of the horses and noticed Cujo was missing," Emma said, her voice cracking with emotion.

"Are you sure he isn't way out there? That's a big pasture...," Michael began, but Emma was shaking her head before he finished.

"I looked, and I thought maybe he was laying down somewhere and I couldn't see him, but I can't find him anywhere," Emma said, fighting the tears threatening to well up. There was no time for tears.

"Let's take the four-wheeler out there and make sure there isn't something we're missing," Michael said, his voice even and reassuring. Emma nodded and a smile tugged at her lips despite the dire situation. Michael had a way of calming her down and making her feel like everything would be ok. Even when it very well may not be.

Emma managed to spit out an "ok" before they headed towards the four-wheeler. Michael climbed into the driver's seat and Emma swung her leg around the backside of the four-wheeler, wrapping her arms around Michael's waist. Had this not been a missing horse situation, she thought about how incredibly romantic this ride would have been.

Michael hit the gas, beelining for the back pasture where Cujo was supposed to be. The other horses in the pasture flung their heads up in surprise momentarily, dropping them back towards the grass when they realized it was just the four-wheeler with familiar people on it. The horses were used to the four-wheeler tearing around the farm when Michael made repairs or did a property fence line check.

Michael hopped off the four-wheeler to swing the gate open. Emma and Michael continued down the far-right side of the pasture, and Emma scanned every inch of it for Cujo, hoping she had simply missed him somehow before.

Emma noticed Michael was checking the fence line for any broken boards as they passed by. So far, he hadn't slowed down, so she assumed he wasn't seeing anything broken. Emma's heart sank a little with each passing minute as they cruised slowly along the back side of the fencing. At this point, Emma had been able to get her eyes on every inch of the pasture with no sign of Cujo.

"He didn't just vanish," she thought. Of course he didn't; more than likely, he was in the back of someone's trailer headed...Emma couldn't even finish that thought. Her stomach churned just thinking about poor Cujo scared and alone wherever he was.

Instead, she focused on the wooden boards beside them, helping Michael check for any sign that the horse may have jumped the pasture fence instead.

They were driving along the final side of the pasture now. Michael was driving even slower, hoping like she was that they would see some sign Cujo had simply escaped. Her throat felt tight as Michael stopped the four-wheeler and shut it off, turning around as far as he could to face her.

"Do you want to check again?" Michael asked softly. His tone implied that he knew Emma was in a fragile emotional state at this point.

Emma bit her lip and nodded, afraid speaking might trigger her to lose control of her teetering emotions. It was not hard to imagine she was Clara and it was her own horse that was suddenly missing.

"Should we call Clara?" Michael asked, his voice even softer than before, one eyebrow raised in concern. Yes, Michael certainly had guessed what was running through her mind.

"Not yet," Emma replied.

Michael nodded and turned back around, starting the four-wheeler's engine.

They scanned the fence line again, even slower this time. Emma wondered if this was a colossal waste of time. After all, they had been pretty thorough the first time. Emma continued to look at each fence board carefully, but her mind was elsewhere.

It was time to reconsider the possibility she had originally come to: Cujo had been stolen. She hoped reevaluating the fence line wasn't diminishing their odds of finding Cujo while he was freshly missing. Fighting that nauseous feeling in her gut again, Emma forced herself to think about her next move.

Calling the police for starters. Well, that was nothing new, she was practically on a first name basis with the police at this point.

Calling Clara...that would be the last thing she did. Having at least some solid information when she made that call would at least help soften the blow.

Was that really it? Was that all she could do? Emma felt helpless. It was a similar feeling to when Mandy had been taken.

"But you found her...," Emma reminded herself. Still, she had gotten lucky. How on earth was she supposed to track down Cujo when she had absolutely no leads? Even the police couldn't find these thieves after weeks of investigation.

Emma's eye suddenly caught a quarter-sized, fresh-looking chip in the top rail of one of the fence boards.

"Stop!" Emma yelled over the four-wheeler's engine.

Michael hit the brakes quickly, and Emma began dismounting before it had completely stopped. Was she imagining things? Or hoping for some sort of miracle that didn't exist?

Jogging over to the small indentation she had seen, Emma leaned in, looking at it closely. Her finger ran over the deviation in the fence board, and she felt the tiny wood hairs of damaged wood on her fingertips. All the fence boards were painted, and it was clear this chip in the wood was recent. It didn't look like it had been rained on or affected by the elements in any way.

"Definitely recent," she thought.

Emma could hear Michael's soft footfalls on the grass behind her.

"What is it?" he asked, leaning in to assess the splintered wood for himself.

"This looks recent," he said, confirming her suspicions.

"What if Cujo jumped the fence and his hoof grazed the board on the way over?" Emma asked, her heartbeat picking up as she thought more about the very real possibility he had just jumped out. It still seemed too good to be true.

"Could be. I did a pretty thorough fence line check yesterday morning and I don't remember seeing it," Michael said, meeting her gaze. Still, they had technically missed it the first time they went down the fence line, so it was possible Michael missed it yesterday too. Was she seeing only what she wanted to see?

"What do you want to do, Emma?" Michael asked, taking her hand in his. Pulling Emma closer to him, he slid one hand around her waist. Emma knew exactly what he meant; call the police and start alerting everyone of Cujo being taken or waste time exploring the slight possibility he jumped the fence.

Emma racked her brain, trying to remember if Clara had ever mentioned Cujo jumping out of pastures before. She came up with nothing. There was no way she was going to call Clara and ask either, only to panic her before they had more information.

Emma loved being Live Oak Farm's barn manager, but this was one of those times she hated the weighted feeling of responsibility and the decisions that responsibility forced her to make. She stood there staring back at Michael, shifting her weight from one foot to the other as she contemplated her decision.

"I think we should look for him first before calling the police and Clara," Emma stated, hoping she sounded sure of her decision. Her gut was telling her it was the best choice; Emma just hoped she wouldn't regret it later.

"Ok, let's look for him," Michael agreed, giving her a kiss on the cheek before walking back toward the four-wheeler. Emma smiled watching Michael walk away from her. With him by her side, she felt like she could face anything. And technically, they already had. After all, this wasn't the first time they had chased down a missing horse, and odds were, it wouldn't be the last.

Emma climbed behind Michael on the four-wheeler. They wound their way out of the pasture, shutting the gate behind them. Michael took the path that led between the pastures, toward the back side of the property that was unfenced. If Cujo was still on this property, odds were he ended up back here. If he was anywhere else, they would have seen him by now. This was the last hope they had of finding him, if he was not stolen, that is.

Emma squinted, trying to see as far out as she could. Her eyes desperately searched for any sign of the dark bay hiding between the rolling hills.

"Emma!" Michael's voice made her heart beat faster. She was already scanning the rolling fields for what he could be referring to but saw nothing. What had Michael seen?

"What is it?" Emma replied quickly. Michael didn't respond at first, instead turning the four-wheeler around, back tracking the way they came.

"There," Michael said, turning off the four-wheeler. Emma's eyes followed the direction Michael's finger was pointing. Then, she saw it too. A large, fresh-looking crack in the fence board bordering their property and the neighboring farm. Could this be it? The possibility she had barely dared to hope for.

"Do you think he could have jumped that fence too?" Michael said, turning around, meeting her gaze.

"It's possible," Emma replied.

"Only one way to find out," Michael said, firing the four-wheeler back up and heading toward the front of the property and out the front gate. They turned onto the back road and then into the driveway of the neighboring farm. Emma was relieved their neighbors did not have a gated entrance as they continued down the long, winding gravel drive.

A short, older woman was sweeping the aisle of a quaint, four stall barn when they pulled up. The woman tilted her head curiously before setting her broom down.

"Sorry to bother you ma'am," Michael said, tipping his ball cap respectfully. "Have you seen a tall, dark bay gelding on your farm today? We live just next door and believe he may have jumped the fence onto your property."

The woman shook her head. "Why, no I haven't, but feel free to look for him," the woman said, motioning towards the back half of her property.

"Thank you," Michael said before quickly hopping back on the four-wheeler where Emma still sat. They drove down the center of the long property. This property was much more narrow than Live Oaks Farm and seemed to go on for miles behind the barn. It was dotted with the same stunning live oaks and rolling hills their farm had. Great for the owners of such a lovely property, not so great for trying to find a potentially missing horse.

They continued driving at a moderate speed, Emma scanning the left side of the farm while Michael searched the right.

"Seriously, how far back does this farm go?" Emma thought as they motored on. Each second they spent looking for him she began regretting her decision. What if she had called the police right away? Maybe they could have caught the person if

she had simply faced the facts staring right in front of her: someone had probably stolen Cujo.

Emma felt the four-wheeler slow down and then come to a stop. Maybe Michael was about to tell her the exact same thing that had been running through her mind for the last few minutes; this was a waste of time.

Michael turned around in his seat, his eyes were lit up and a smile stretched across his face. Emma froze, digesting the meaning of the look. Her eyes darted to the fields around them.

There, a little ways away, was a very content looking Cujo grazing in their neighbor's yard like he was supposed to be there. Emma found herself laughing and then crying.

"Cujo!" she called out.

The dark bay lifted his head, his ears swiveling in their direction. The look on his face was so casual like he was thinking, "oh, finally you've come to get me. Isn't it past my dinner time?" Emma laughed again, relieved he seemed completely unharmed, and most importantly, he was not in the back of a thief's trailer.

Emma walked over to Cujo, slipping a halter and lead rope over his head, giving his neck a quick pat before leading him over to the four-wheeler.

Michael was standing next to the four-wheeler now, grinning ear to ear. He looked just about as happy as she felt. Cujo had simply escaped; he hadn't been stolen, thankfully.

"You caused us quite the scare, buddy," Michael murmured to the gelding, patting him. Cujo seemed more interested in snagging a few more mouthfuls of grass than anything else.

Emma shook her head, still reeling from the last hour or so.

"Thanks for helping me find him," Emma said to Michael, who was looking right at her now.

"I guess finding lost horses is kind of our thing now," Michael teased. Before she could say anything in response, Michael stepped closer to her, wrapping his arms around the hollow of her back.

"You know how much I care about you, right?" he said, pulling her closer.

Emma felt her heart flutter, and Michael leaned in to kiss her. Of course, Michael's actions had proven how much he cared about her. But hearing him say hit her in a different way emotionally.

Electricity shot through her the moment his lips grazed hers and the rest of the world seemed to fade to black. He deepened the kiss, and Emma let herself get lost in the way his lips felt against hers.

Emma felt a slight tug of the lead rope as Cujo reached for grass just past where the rope would let him go, bringing her back to reality. Emma pulled away from Michael slowly, a slight smile on her face.

"I guess we should get this guy back home," Emma said reluctantly. It felt kind of nice being all alone with Michael acres away from anyone else.

"We probably should," Michael agreed, but his hands lingered on her hips.

They both stood there a moment longer, holding one another's gaze.

Another tug at the lead rope almost knocked Emma off balance this time, causing her to finally look away.

"Alright Cujo, let's get you back home and let your mom know what you've been up to today," Emma said, shooting an affectionate glance at the horse who was reaching as far as he could towards a patch of grass he clearly thought looked better than the grass directly in front of him.

Michael swung his leg over the four-wheeler and Emma climbed on behind him, holding the lead rope out so Cujo could walk beside it.

On the way back, Emma called Clara, filling her in on her horse's little expedition to the neighboring farm. Clara laughed, and thanked Emma for tracking him down and bringing him home safe and sound.

It was certainly a much better call than Emma had expected to make earlier that day.

"Did Clara say why Cujo might have jumped to fence?" Michael asked when she hung up the phone.

"Apparently he really hates the sound of gunshots. Clara said one other time he jumped the fence when he was still at Frank's farm, where she is a working student. One of his sons decided to turn the back part of the farm into a makeshift shooting range."

Michael paused, then turned around slightly with his eyes wide.

"I heard gunshots today, come to think of it. They came from somewhere across the street maybe? It went on for about fifteen minutes, right around the time you were at the house for lunch," Michael replied.

Well, there it was. Mystery solved. Poor Cujo's fear of gunshots sent him launching over every fence to get away from the spooky sound, which apparently meant going to the furthest corner of the neighbor's farm.

They slowly made their way back to the farm with Cujo walking casually along trying to snag another bite of grass now and then. Emma recalled Michael's words not so long ago stating he wanted to take things slow. However, after the moment they just had, it felt like something much more serious was happening between them.

Chapter Eleven

Emma had waited for this day for what felt like forever.

But finally, the day had come. Today, they were Miami-bound.

Thoughts of sparkling ocean waves crashing in the background as horses, and one horse she adored in particular, leaped incredibly large jumps at an intensely fast pace. She was excited just thinking about it.

Emma was sure the drive down there would feel endless as the slowly passing miles took her closer to a place she had wanted to visit for some time now, and to an event that had only been a dream to attend. The first time she heard about this competition was years ago back in Ohio. One of the girls at Maggie's barn had been raving about it after her parents took her as a birthday present. Emma watched video after video with her barn friends, wondering what it must be like to attend that event in person. After all, it combined three of Emma's favorite things in the world: horses, show jumping, and the ocean.

Emma folded another tank top and set it on top of the overflowing suitcase. Sure, they only planned to be away maybe four or five days tops, but overpacking was one of those fatal flaws she could never seem to get past. No matter how many times she said to herself, "I really shouldn't have packed this much for such a short trip," Emma still found herself packing way more than she could ever possibly wear. After all, you just never know what you're going to want to wear until the day of.

Pushing on the top part of her suitcase in order to get it to zip, Emma looked up just as the zipper finished its struggle to the other side. Michael stood in the open doorway of her bedroom, arms folded across his chest with an amused look on his face. Emma blushed reflexively.

"You know how long we will actually be away, right?" Michael teased, sarcasm dripping from each word.

Emma tossed Michael a look that made it clear she was perfectly aware.

"I like to be prepared," she stated, holding her chin a little higher as she stuck to her story. Technically, that was true, and in this case, prepared meant bringing half of her closet.

"Sure," Michael replied, sarcasm still lingering in his tone.

Emma smiled despite his words. The impending trip made it impossible to be anything but ecstatic.

"I pulled the truck around; I had a feeling you would not be packing lightly," Michael said, smiling and winking her way.

"Very funny, Michael," Emma shot back.

Michael grabbed the handle of her suitcase, pulling it off the bed. Emma had learned by now not to argue with Michael about things like helping her with her bags or opening the car door herself. He always insisted, and she had finally given up trying to tell him otherwise. Secretly, his gentlemanly charm was one of the things she liked best about him, despite her deep seeded independent horse-girl spirit.

"Be right back," Emma said to Michael as he loaded her bags into the back of the truck. She sprinted across the lawn toward the barn.

Jogging a little slower now as she entered the barn, she stopped short at Valentine's stall.

"You behave for Sam and be a good girl when Clara rides you this week, ok?" Emma murmured to her mare.

Valentine's ears swiveled forward in the direction of her owner's voice. Emma planted a long kiss on Valentine's nose, giving her one last pet and the half-crumbled treat that was still in her pocket from earlier that day.

Jogging back to the truck, she saw Michael waiting patiently by the now open passenger side door.

"Saying one last goodbye to Valentine?" he asked, although he said it more as a statement. Michael knew her all too well by now.

"Of course," Emma said, offering him a warm smile as she climbed into the truck.

Michael hopped into the driver's side and put the already running truck in gear as they headed out the farm's black iron gates. Emma looked in the sideview mirror as the farm slowly faded from view. Even with such exciting days ahead of her, she still had a hard time leaving the farm and the horse she cared for.

As predicted, the miles rolled by slowly as they made their way down the coast towards south Florida. It still sometimes blew her mind just how different the terrain was in south Florida versus Ocala. Back home, she remembered taking a trip from Ohio to Michigan for a concert. If someone had blindfolded her and stuck her in Michigan, which was four hours from her hometown, she probably wouldn't even know she had left her home state. Only about four hours apart here and Ocala and south Florida were like different worlds.

As each hour passed, Emma watched the rolling hills and live oaks turn into palm trees and that lush tropical foliage found this far south.

Finally, Emma watched as Michael pulled into the parking lot of the hotel. Of course, Emma had asked where they were staying, but Michael had been tight lipped about it.

Now, Emma understood why. The Miami hotel he had chosen was directly on the beach.

Emma felt a surge of emotion rush through her. Michael had surprised her in a similar way once before when they had taken a trip together earlier in the year. That was a much different situation, of course, since Michael was still just a friend, and she was dating Liam at the time. His thoughtfulness about the oceanfront restaurant he had chosen to take her to, though, had been the beginning of her suspicions of Michael's feelings for her. If she was honest with herself, it was a moment that had begun to slowly change how she saw Michael as well.

"Michael," Emma said, almost breathlessly.

"Do you like it?" Michael spoke softly, and his eyes met hers. He seemed to be waiting for her approval.

Emma paused, looking for words that conveyed how his gesture made her feel. Every word choice that crossed her mind fell flat. There was only one thing that might be able to show him exactly how she felt.

Emma unbuckled her seatbelt and leaned across the center console. Her hand gently wrapped around the back of his neck, her fingers running through the hair peeking out from under his ball cap. Her lips pressed against his firmly, moving slowly. She pulled him closer, sliding even further across the truck as the kiss become more passionate with each passing second. Emma felt her head spinning as his fingers brushed lightly across her cheek.

She pulled back, a slight smirk on her face.

"I hope that answers your question," Emma said, feeling quite certain she had relayed the message effectively.

Michael pulled her back in briefly giving her a peck on the cheek.

"I think you made your point," Michael said, a goofy grin lingering on his lips.

Emma was sure this was going to be a weekend she would never forget.

Michael grabbed their bags from the car, and they headed into the lobby of the hotel. The tall ceilings with gold detailed design and a crystal chandelier caught her eye as they headed to the desk to check in.

"Here is your room key, sir. You'll be in room two hundred," the concierge said with a smile, handing Michael the card wrapped in an envelope.

Michael thanked the concierge and they headed down the hall to their room. The hotel room door swung open, exposing a boutique style room décor and two queen beds. No surprise, of course. Michael had proven time and again he was a gentleman at his core.

"Dibs on the bed by the window!" Emma called out, all but launching herself onto the bed. She stretched her arms out, almost letting out a soft moan as her skin touched the soft sheets. This bed felt like she was laying on a cloud.

Michael put his hands up in defeat after setting down their bags. He walked casually over to the window that ran across the entire back wall of their room. He pulled back the curtains, revealing their view from the hotel room.

Emma gasped out loud, her jaw dropping slightly at the breathtaking view. Michael had booked a room with what she could only assume was one of the best views of the ocean.

Slowly getting up for the cloud-like bed, Emma walked wide-eyed towards the window, pressing her fingertips against the glass. She felt Michael's arms slowly twist around her waist, his head resting gently on her shoulder. Emma's cheek rested against his as she stared out at the tide rolling in and out in front of them.

The color of the water this far south was stunning. Even from here, she could see the bottom of the sand-colored shallow end that slowly gave way to a light blue hue that got darker the further out she looked.

Emma stood there staring at the water, soaking it all in while wrapped in Michael's arms. It was one of those perfect moments she knew would linger in her mind for a very long time.

Emma tossed aside another top that didn't meet her criteria.

Normally, she couldn't care less what she put on. After all, her life revolved around working with horses, and whatever she wore was destined to be covered in hay, dirt, tack soap, and horsehair, at the very least.

But an event of this caliber required just the right thing to wear. Unfortunately, she had not found exactly what that was yet in her suitcase. As predicted, she had slept like a log in the insanely comfortable bed and felt a buzz of energy fueled by a good night's rest and the day's excitement.

Tossing yet another vetoed outfit choice on the bed beside her, Emma let out a soft sigh. Michael made a snort laugh sound on the other bed across the room.

"You packed almost everything you own, how is it possible you can't find anything to wear," Michael teased, watching as Emma continued to dig through her suitcase.

Emma shot Michael a look that made him laugh.

Finally, Emma reluctantly decided on something to wear and freshened up quickly in the bathroom.

"Ready!" Emma said, emerging from the bathroom as she slid on her sandals.

Michael's eyes swept over her, widening slightly.

He walked over to her, slipping his fingers through hers and kissing her on the cheek.

"You look stunning," he murmured inches away from her ear, sending a shiver down her body.

They headed out of the room, hand in hand, towards the lobby of the hotel. Emma practically skipped the entire way. She felt giddy knowing she was a short drive from the long-anticipated event with Michael by her side.

Emma began walking towards the parking garage where the truck was parked, but felt Michael squeeze her hand, gently tugging her in the opposite direction. She looked over at him with a quizzical expression.

"It's walking distance," Michael said, answering her unspoken question. A smile was tugging at the corner of his lip and there was a look in his eyes Emma couldn't quite place, like he was holding something back.

Michael led the way toward the back of the hotel, and they exited through the glass sliding doors. The smell of pool water immediately wafted around Emma as they walked past a small tiki bar area and then rounded the corner to where the pool came into view.

But the sweet smell of sand baking in the sun and ocean water began overwhelming her senses. Emma couldn't see it though, since the hotel's outdoor area was surrounded by thick, tropical plants and palm trees. Michael seemed to know where he was going as he led her down a sandy path that was still surrounded by the tropical plants and trees that made it impossible to tell where they were going. Knowing Michael, he had called down to the front desk while she was getting ready to find out the quickest way to the event.

Suddenly the path took a sharp turn and opened up to a wooden boardwalk that looked like it ran miles down the beach, parallel to the ocean.

"This is incredible," Emma said in a breathy tone as they headed down the boardwalk.

"I thought you would prefer the twelve-minute boardwalk stroll along the beach to a five-minute drive," Michael replied, seeming pleased with his decision.

"I mean, why would anyone want to drive and miss a walk like this?" Emma said, her eyes darting between the water to her right and the palm tree lined boardwalk ahead of them.

Emma was enjoying their walk down the boardwalk so much she was almost surprised when she realized they had arrived at the event. It was true what they said about time flying. For Emma, every moment she spent oceanside seemed to be in fast-forward.

Michael pulled the tickets from his pocket and handed them to the man standing at the entrance. Emma remembered Michael mentioning that due to the caliber of the event, they wouldn't be able to go to the backside of the stables or warm-up ring like they normally would to say hi to Jenn and Jimmie John.

As they climbed high up into the grandstands, Emma was able to catch a glimpse of horses being walked past the entrance of the ring. Somewhere back there was her beloved Jimmie John. He had grown into the exceptional Grand Prix horse she always knew he could be, and Emma felt honored to have been a part of his life even for a short while.

As they settled into their seats, Emma took in the sensational view in front of them. To her right was the entrance to the ring and the covered VIP seating area that ran along the long side of the arena. Emma imagined Liza and David Williams were siting somewhere in there as they were majority owners of Jimmie John.

To her left was the glistening blue-white ocean waves crashing against the sand. Beach bystanders had already began gathering along this side of the arena. Some looked like that had been intentionally camped out there for some time while others seemed simply curious about the monumental looking jumps and horses competing directly on the beach.

In front of them she could see for miles down the beach. Hotels of various sizes and caliber winded down the coast. Emma may have wanted to come to this event for the horses, but she was shocked at just how gorgeous the views were from this beachside grandstand.

Emma turned to Michael, smiling widely. His eyes met hers, his finger gently hooked under her chin and his lips softly covered hers briefly. She felt the electricity of his touch surge through her. Emma closed her eyes, soaking up the perfect moment she was living in.

A perfect moment that lasted all of fifteen seconds.

Seconds after Emma opened her eyes, she saw someone waving frantically at her from the VIP tented area. Sitting at the furthest table over, and in a direct line of vision to her and Michael, sat Cathy and Liam.

Emma suddenly felt on display, her cheeks flushing red hot. She froze, wondering how long they had been sitting there and how much they had seen. A hundred questions raced through her mind. What would Cathy say about her and Michael, two of her employees, being in a relationship without saying anything to her first? How bad would it hurt Liam seeing them together after everything that had gone down between them?

Emma swallowed hard, knowing she needed to do something soon. Anything, besides stare like a deer in the headlights back at them. Her hand slowly raised, waving back sheepishly. Emma saw Cathy motioning for her to come over in response.

Michael was looking over at her now, watching the panic-stricken expression cross her face, and he followed her eyes until he saw why Emma was looking like she had just seen a ghost. Ghost of boyfriends past, one could say.

"Oh boy," Michael murmured, barely moving his lips. He also waved over in Cathy and Liam's direction politely. Cathy was still motioning for them to come over, standing up in her chair now.

"I think we need to go over there," Emma said through her teeth, barely moving her lips as well.

"We don't really have a choice, do we," Michael replied quietly, more as a statement than a question.

Emma and Michael stood up very slowly, making their way through their row and down the grandstand stairs. Emma had not seen Cathy in what felt like forever. She missed the woman that had come to be like family to her, and had it just been Cathy here today, it would be a different story. But poor Liam sat uncomfortably next to his aunt after witnessing the public display of affection between his ex-almost-fiancé and the guy that he believed ruined their relationship. Awkward didn't begin to cover what kind of conversation this was about to be.

It didn't seem to matter that Emma had walked at a snail's pace, because they were standing next to the tented area what felt like seconds later. Cathy walked down the small flight of stairs that led from the VIP tent to the main spectator area. Liam reluctantly followed behind Cathy; his gaze fixated on the ground.

"My dear, Emma!" Cathy exclaimed with her usual enthusiasm, sweeping Emma into a hug and kissing her on the cheek. Emma smiled warmly back at Cathy, genuinely happy to see her. Emma decided not to let her gaze drift to Liam who stood just behind her. Emma felt bad for Michael who stood inches from her, probably feeling even more awkward than she was.

Cathy turned her attention to Michael now. Emma turned toward Michael too as Cathy pulled Michael in for a hug.

"I hope you are doing well, Michael?" Cathy asked, not a trace of awkwardness in her voice, as if she had not just seen him and Emma cozied up beside one another moments before.

"Maybe they didn't see as much as I thought?" she thought.

"I'm doing well Cathy, thank you for asking," Michael replied, his voice steadier than Emma would have expected.

Liam finally looked up and his eyes met Emma's. A wave of guilt and nausea flooded her as she looked back at the man she once knew so intimately. There was something about seeing an ex for the first time after breaking up that seemed to trigger every kind of emotion. This situation, in particular, was a heightened version of that as she stood next to Michael who was now her boyfriend, and in Liam's mind, the reason they broke up in the first place.

"Hey, Liam," Emma said as casually as she could manage, but her voice cracked as she tried to get the words out.

"Smooth," she thought.

A brief look of discontent crossed Liam's face.

"Hi Emma," he replied in a cold tone.

"Well, this isn't going well," she thought.

Liam glanced Michael's way once, his forehead and the area between his eyes were scrunched up a bit, but he said nothing to Michael and shoved his hands in his pockets instead. Michael cleared his throat and shifted his weight.

For five long seconds, no one spoke.

"So, are you guys together now or something?" Liam stated, a hint of bitterness rang in his words.

Ouch. Emma felt like someone had stabbed her in the gut. It was safe to say Liam and Cathy had seen the affection between her and Michael after all. Emma's jaw dropped slightly in surprise at Liam's bold statement. The tension in the air around the four of them could have been cut with a knife.

Cathy shot Liam a look of disapproval. The air hung heavy while Emma scrambled to think of something to say that didn't sound like she was rubbing their relationship in his face.

"We are," Michael's voice stated softly behind her before she could come up with anything to say herself. She felt Michael's fingertips gently graze the back of her shirt as he rested his hand lightly on the small of her back. Emma was sure it was meant to be reassuring to her, but all she could think about was the pain that was probably causing Liam whose eyes had already darted to where Michael's hand lay.

Emma took one small step towards Liam and Michael's hand fell back to his side.

"I'm sorry you had to find out this way," Emma said, first glancing at Liam then Cathy. Really, she intended the statement toward them both. Emma had been meaning to call Cathy and tell her before she found out accidently, like this. Especially since she and Michael were still co-workers, and it was at Cathy's farm where they worked.

Liam's gaze continued to bore into her, but he made no effort to respond.

Cathy offered a polite smile and rested one hand on Emma's upper arm. "It's ok, I understand dear," Cathy replied. It seemed like Cathy meant that, and perhaps she was trying to keep her response neutral since she stood a foot away from her clearly still heartbroken nephew. Emma made a mental note to talk to Cathy about it later, one on one. Emma wasn't sure how else to respond now, so she smiled half-heartedly back at Cathy.

After another couple seconds of awkward silence, Cathy cleared her throat.

"Are you still planning to spend some time in Wellington this week after the Miami event?" Cathy asked Emma.

"Yes, I figured since I was this far south already, I may as well spend time with some of my old Wellington friends and watch a few horses I know compete. Jimmie John has another Grand Prix later in the week in Wellington as well, so I figured it was a good excuse to stay south a few more days," Emma replied. She decided it was best not to use terms like "we" at his point, even though it was probably obvious Michael would be with her.

"Well, don't be a stranger dear! Promise you will stop by the house and see me at least once? I would like to take you to dinner while you're in town as well," Cathy said. The mood seemed to lighten a little as Emma and Cathy made plans for the upcoming days.

"I will let you head back to your seats; it looks like the event is about to start," Emma said, watching one of the security officers clearing the entrance to the arena.

"It was nice running into you, honey! See you later this week," Cathy said waving them off.

"You too Cathy, see you soon," Emma said quickly before turning on her heels back towards the grandstand seats. Still, she managed to accidentally catch one last somber look from Liam before they turned away.

Emma wished she hadn't, knowing it would haunt her the rest of the day at the very least. Breaking Liam's heart had never been her intention, and it had broken her own heart to do it.

Emma and Michael sat back down in their seats, but the mood had certainly shifted from the bliss she had been feeling before. Emma looked over, feeling

Michael's gaze on her. She smiled at him hoping it would throw him off. The last thing she wanted was to drag Michael down too. After all, he had spent so much time and money planning this trip to make her happy.

The announcer's voice pulled her from her thoughts, stating the first horse and rider's name and a few facts about them. Emma decided to push Liam's expression from her mind and enjoy the event. There was nothing she could have done to make him feel better anyway, she reminded herself.

After a couple of riders had taken their turn on course, Emma began enjoying herself, holding her breath each time a horse took a bad spot and cheering as each of them landed off the final fence. The salted ocean breeze blowing through her hair and the impressive horse and rider athletes held her, and the run in with Liam finally slipped her mind.

"Next on course is Freaky Fast ridden by Jennifer Meyers, owned by the Twin Oaks Syndicate," the announcer's voice echoed across the grandstand. Emma stood up reflexively at the announcement of their names, clapping and cheering loudly as Jenn tried to keep the now jigging Jimmie John at bay long enough to wait for the buzzer to sound.

Emma grinned widely watching Jimmie John canter off with power towards the first jump. He boldly leaped into the air, and Emma couldn't believe she had been lucky enough to so much as warm up a horse like him. His form over the monumental sized fences looked improved even from the last time she saw him compete. It was clear Jenn had been working hard to prepare him for this high caliber event. He truly looked like he belonged here amongst the best of the best.

Jenn turned her head and sat back as she legged up Jimmie John to the third fence.

"He's doing so well," Emma whispered under her breath, afraid if she said it too loudly it would somehow jinx the horse.

They were over halfway through the course now. Emma's death grip on the seat in front of her tuned her knuckles white. Jimmie John was still jumping clear, and so far they had no faults.

The muscles under his dark coat bunched as he pushed off the ground over a wide oxer. Sometimes Emma wondered how these animals were able to clear such impressive jumps with a rider on their back. Horses held a power that left her forever mystified by them.

There were only two jumps left of the course. If Jimmie John cleared them both, he would have a completely clear round within the optimum time, they would move on to the jump off later. Emma held her breath and counted strides in her head as they approached the final combination. A wrong move on the first jump would make it easy to knock a pole on the second fence.

Jimmie came in strong, as usual, and seemed to get faster as he went on. The gelding took a slight stutter step that had Emma gasping, but he managed to clear the jump anyway. Jenn sat deep in the saddle, getting the horse to balance on his back end and not take the next fence too early.

Jimmie John flew over the final fence in what felt like slow motion, landing off of it with a head shake. He always seemed to know when he had done a good job.

Emma yelled and clapped, jumping up and down as she watched Jenn smile radiantly and pat the dark bay gelding's neck. Emma turned back toward Michael, whose smile reflected hers.

It was certainly a day she would never forget.

Chapter Twelve

"I can't believe he placed third in a competition like that!" Emma said, excitement still leaking into her tone. She shook her head, almost in disbelief.

Michael walked beside her on the boardwalk, smiling over at Emma and her child-like enthusiasm as they headed back to their hotel. When it came to horses, Emma's inner child came pouring out.

"He has come such a long way from the first day he came to Twin Oaks," Michael replied.

"How long had he been at Twin Oaks before I arrived?" Emma asked curiously.

"Oh, maybe two years? He was pretty green, and I remember Jenn saying that he was 'a lot of horse,' but that she saw so much potential in him. Looks like she was right," Michael said thoughtfully.

Emma had met many horses over the years that fit that description. She recalled an off-the-track Thoroughbred Maggie had purchased that was quite challenging to retrain. Maggie always swore there was something about her that was special, and that horse ended up being her division winning show jumper several years in a row. It just went to show that some horses needed a little time than others.

They fell silent as they walked along in the dark with just the dim lanterns lighting the boardwalk in front of them. The invisible, crashing waves in the distance triggered something in Emma's mind that she had been suppressing for the last several hours: Liam.

The look on Liam's face flashed through her thoughts, making her feel guilty all over again. Michael had his fingers intertwined in hers as they walked along, which for some reason only made her feel guiltier. Emma was blissfully happy with Michael, and Liam was miserable because of it. Emma gently pulled her hand free of Michael's. He stopped walking, turning toward her with a confused expression.

"Is everything ok?" he asked.

It made sense, her suddenly pulling away from his touch with what she imagined was a pained look on her face. Emma never had been any good at hiding her emotions, and he was probably reading her like a book.

Emma sighed audibly. She leaned against the wood railing of the boardwalk, running her fingers through her hair.

"I feel bad about Liam seeing us today," Emma said softly. Michael leaned against the railing next to Emma, wrapping an arm around her shoulders.

"I figured it might have something to do with that. You looked pretty torn up about it after we headed back to our seats," Michael replied.

"The look on his face...Michael, I hurt him so badly," Emma said, fighting tears that she felt stinging the corners of her eyes.

"Let's say I wasn't in the picture. Do you think things would have worked out between the two of you?"

Emma shot Michael a concerned look. What exactly was he getting at? She paused to think a moment, really considering his question.

"No. I don't think we wanted the same things, honestly. I would have been unhappy in Wellington knowing I had given up my dream job, and he would have been unhappy in Ocala away from his own dream job, his friends, and his aunt."

"So, do you regret your decision then?" Michael asked, softer this time.

"No, of course not," Emma replied quickly. "I'm happy with you, and I think it was the best thing for both Liam and I to split up," Emma added.

"Well, then, there you go. You need to remember that whatever pain he is in now will eventually fade. You did what was best for you both, like you said. Try not to beat yourself up over it, ok?" Michael said, his fingers running gently across her arm.

"You're right," Emma agreed. Already she felt the heaviness of the guilt she was feeling begin to lift away. She and Liam became a ticking timebomb the moment she took Cathy's job offer and decided to stay in Ocala, and in some ways, she had known that from the beginning.

"And for the record, I'm happy with you too," Michael replied. He pushed off the railing as he turned to face her. He grabbed the rail behind her, his arms on either side of her. His body leaned in close, gently pushing her up against the rail. Emma smiled mischievously, wrapping her arms around her neck, leaning in closer until her face was but an inch from his.

Her lips brushed against his lightly, then his pressed more firmly against hers as the kiss quickly turned passionate. His body lay against hers more firmly now. Suddenly, Emma felt her feet leave the ground as Michael picked her up, setting her on top of the wood railing, his lips never leaving hers. She leaned down from where she was now sitting on the rail, lost in a kiss that took her breath away, shooting electricity from her head to her toes. Fireworks could have gone off behind them, and it still wouldn't hold a candle to the kiss they were sharing.

Emma was not sure how long they had been there, lost in the kiss, when Michael finally pulled away. His hands cupped her cheeks gently, his eyes locked directly on hers. He looked at her like no one had ever looked at her before: like in that moment, the two of them were lost in their own little world.

"Emma Walker, I love you," Michael said, his eyes never leaving hers. Emma caught her breath, sliding off the railing and landing on her feet, a little surprised by his words. It wasn't so long ago he was telling her he wanted to take things slow. When had he had a change of heart?

"Are you sure?" Emma blurted out without thinking. Whoops. Probably not the ideal question after someone tells you they love you.

Michael smiled warmly at her despite her question, his arms wrapping around the hollow of her back. "I've never been more sure of anything."

His green eyes sparkled, reflecting his words. Emma had no doubt he meant everything he was saying now. Emma smiled back, considering how she had been feeling about Michael for quite some time now.

"Michael Hale, I love you too," Emma said, still smiling as she spoke.

This felt very different from the last time when Liam had told her that he loved her. It felt, well, *right* this time. Michael had been her friend for a long time, and she had felt like she had been falling in love with him since the moment she had chosen to be with him. Maybe even before that if she was honest with herself.

Michael leaned in again, pressing his lips to hers. The kiss felt softer this time, more intimate.

Emma's body pressed against Michael's, and she once again found herself lost in the kiss.

Palm trees blurred by as they drove up the Florida state route.

After a couple days of sun and sand in Miami, they were now headed up the coast towards Wellington. Emma wasn't sure she could remember a time in her life she had been happier than she was now. Michael's fingers were laced through hers as they drove down the road.

It felt funny to be back in Wellington under such different circumstances. The last time she was here she had broken up with Liam. My, how things had changed since then!

Still, she had so many fond memories with Michael here too, when they had both been there working for Twin Oaks. He had already promised her dinner at the local Mexican restaurant that had become their favorite while they worked in town.

Emma sent a message to Cathy, letting her know they had safely arrived in town. Cathy had already been going out of her way to make sure Emma knew that she had no problem with her and Michael's relationship. That was something Emma had been beyond relieved about. Cathy had even dropped hints about how she wasn't surprised and saw this coming. Emma wasn't entirely sure how to feel about that, so she held on to the fact that her and Michael's boss was approving of their relationship. Still, Emma wondered if Cathy would always wish she and Liam would have worked out. When she had been with Liam, Cathy had never been shy about making her feelings on that known.

"We're here!" Michael said, pulling Emma from her thoughts and the scenery she had been staring at through the passenger side window. She turned her gaze to the view in front of the truck's windshield. Michael had found a cute hotel tucked in the heart of Wellington, close to both the horse show and some of their favorite local places.

Michael checked in and they put their bags in the hotel room.

"Ready to head to dinner?" Michael asked. They hadn't had anything since breakfast and at this point, an early dinner sounded perfect.

"Absolutely," Emma agreed, grabbing her purse from the hotel's bed.

They got back in the truck and headed to one of the local taverns that had what Michael had considered the best food in Wellington. Emma, of course, made it clear that she shared a different opinion and that the best food in Wellington was still the Mexican restaurant they had frequented.

"Alright, truce!" Michael said with a laugh, pulling into a parking space of the tavern parking lot. They had spent the better part of the drive over debating the two restaurants' pro's and con's. Emma smiled, taking that as a sign of his defeat.

"Mexican restaurant one, tavern zero," she teased.

"If that's how you are taking it...," Michael mumbled under his breath. Not low enough for Emma's excellent hearing though.

Emma shoved him playfully, causing Michael to turn in her direction with a mischievous look on his face. Michael wrapped her up in his arms, lifting her off the ground. Emma squealed in protest until he put her down.

"Fine! Truce!" Emma finally agreed, laughing breathlessly.

Emma couldn't help but think they still felt like the old Emma and Michael; the way they were when they were still best friends before the complications of their relationship threatened to drive them apart. Only now, they had a romantic side on top of the friendship that remained. In her opinion, it was the perfect combination.

The hostess sat them at a table on the far side of the outdoor patio. There was a nice view of the cluster of palm trees that sat across from the restaurant.

Michael set his menu down thirty seconds after reading it. Emma eyed him curiously, prompting a shrug from Michael.

"I know what I like from this place," he replied to her unspoken question, offering her a goofy grin that made her smirk at him.

"I can tell," she replied sarcastically before studying her menu again.

Emma had to admit, this place did have a killer patio. It had been the reason Michael had talked her into eating here in the first place.

The waitress came back over and took their order. Emma and Michael chatted about their plans for the week as they waited for their food. But there was still something that had been circling Emma's thoughts for days now. Sitting here in front of Michael as they sipped casually on the drinks in front of them, her mind ran over that same question. Now she didn't have a slew of fun activities and the beach, like they had in Miami, to keep her from mulling over it endlessly. Like she was right now.

Michael tilted his head to the side, studying her facial expressions.

"What are you thinking about?" he asked.

Busted.

Emma bit her lip. She had considered not asking the question at all and just leaving things the way they were. They were both happy and in love. Why question it? But Emma figured at this point she may not be able to keep it to herself. After all, it seemed to keep running through her thoughts every so often. May as well rip off the band-aid and get the answer she was dying to know.

"I'm just wondering something," Emma began, pausing to decide the best way to word what she wanted to say. "When you told me you loved me the other day, I guess I just wondered what changed. It wasn't so long ago you were warning me you wanted to take things slow," Emma said softly, searching Michael's face for clues to how he might be taking her question.

Michael leaned further back in his chair, crossing his arms across his chest. A smile tugged at the corners of his lips.

"I had a feeling you might bring that up at some point," Michael said, chuckling a little afterwards.

"You did?" Emma was curious now too.

"Oh, yeah. You asking me if I was sure and then not pressing for any further details? I knew it would only be a matter of time before you asked me what changed," Michael grinned widely now, seeming proud of himself for predicting her so well.

He was right, of course.

"Do you want me to tell you that you were right," Emma said in a teasing tone, leaning across the table, holding Michael's gaze.

"Actually, that would be great," he teased back.

"Fine. You were right. Now do I get the answer to my question?" Emma asked.

"I suppose that's fair," Michael replied, still grinning. He paused purposefully, and Emma stared him down until he answered her question.

"It's simple, really. I had every intention of taking things slow. I knew there was a lot at stake because of our history and our friendship on the line. Plus, of course, our working relationship would have been affected if we rushed into things and they fell apart. The problem with that plan was that I started falling in love with you a long time ago. So, when we officially got together, those feelings came back quickly, and it was only a matter of time before I couldn't hold back anymore and told you how I felt."

Emma's heart swelled. She looked at him, the best friend she had also fallen in love with and realized her own feelings had a very similar story.

She leaned over further, and he was leaning across the table too, closing the gap between them. Emma pressed her lips briefly to his, but her face lingered close to his after she pulled away, their eyes locked.

Now, she was quite sure her decision to come to Florida was the best decision she had ever made.

Emma and Michael strolled down the palm tree lined path of Palm Beach Equestrian Center. Emma looked around, smiling at the familiar setting. She recalled getting lost on her first day here.

It was mid-evening, and the sun was getting lower in the sky. Emma knew there were some of the larger show jumping classes going on in the Grand Prix arena today, a few of which had horses she knew competing in them. They had been sitting in the grandstands watching for a couple hours now, and Emma had suggested they stop and see Jimmie John where he was stabled on their way out for the night.

She knew when he competed in the Grand Prix later that week it would be harder to get a chance to spend a few minutes of quality time with him, since he would be prepping for the event. It seemed like far too long ago that she had been able to spend a little one on one time with a horse as special to her as Jimmie John was.

"Where did you say he was stabled again?" Michael asked as they approached the show barns.

"I think Jenn said they are one barn over from where they used to stall," Emma replied.

This was her favorite time of day when the sun began to fade and the heat with it. Michael wrapped an arm around her, and she smiled at him.

As they walked past what used to be the barn they had stabled at when they worked at Twin Oaks, Emma felt a strange sense of coming full circle.

"Is that it?" Michael asked, pointing toward the barn next to them.

"I think so," Emma replied, scrolling back through the messages Jenn had sent about where they were stabled. "Yep, barn thirty-eight, that's it," she confirmed.

They walked towards the barn, and Emma saw a familiar horse head pop out of a stall door. It made her feel good that some of the Twin Oaks horses might still remember her. The horse let out a low, familiar nicker. The other horses in the row of stalls popped their heads out of their stalls to see if they were missing anything exciting.

Emma ran her hand up Stephanie's horse's forelock, patting him on the neck. She made a mental note to see how the young rider was doing and maybe watch her ride before they left Wellington. Emma continued down the line of stalls with Michael just behind her. Some of the horses were ones she knew from working at Twin Oaks; others were new faces of new project horses or boarders.

Emma stopped short, turning around to look behind her. Had she missed Jimmie's stall? She walked back to the beginning of the stalls, this time looking at the stall cards as she went.

When she reached the end of the row of stalls again, she saw Jimmie's name on the very last stall. She peered in, remembering how Jimmie John liked to curl up like a cat and take naps in the evenings.

Her heart stopped, then beat faster at the realization his stall was empty. She controlled her breathing; there was no need to panic. She was sure one of the grooms or the new working student had pulled him out to lunge or canter him around. But why latch his stall back up? That rubbed her the wrong way; it just didn't make any sense.

Emma pulled her phone from her pocket and called Jenn.

"Hey, Jenn! Is any of your staff still at the show grounds?" Emma asked as calmly as she could manage.

"No, everyone should be gone for the day. They left about a half hour ago. Is everything ok?" Jenn asked on the other line.

Emma felt lightheaded the moment she heard Jenn's words over the phone and caught herself from almost dropping it on the ground.

"Jenn, it's Jimmie John...he isn't in his stall," Emma said, her words coming out stammered. She felt the blood drain from her face as she spoke.

"Are you sure?!" Jenn said, panic ringing in her words.

"I'm sure," Emma said, staring into Jimmie's stall.

Jenn excused herself before all but hanging up the phone on Emma, stating she needed to call the police right away. Emma put her phone back in her pocket, her face sheet white. Michael was staring at her, wide-eyed, listening to her conversation and processing the same information she was.

There was no doubt about it this time. Jimmie had been stolen.

"They must have heard about how well he placed in Miami," Emma mumbled. She wasn't even sure if Michael heard her.

Her mind was going a mile a minute, thinking of how this could have happened. There was no way he could have been taken all that long ago. After all, Jenn said on the phone her staff had maybe only left half an hour ago. The place would still have been bustling with people until, well, pretty much right now.

Emma's mind suddenly locked in on that bit of information. What if he was still here? Clearly it would be insanely obvious to have a horse trailer parked in front of the horse barns and load him there. They would have hand-walked him to wherever they parked the trailer, and who would bat an eye at someone walking a horse around? People hand-walked the horses here in the evenings all the time.

There were not many places in the front of the grounds to park a trailer that wouldn't be easily spotted. The streets leading up to the show grounds wouldn't work either; you couldn't just park a trailer on the road around here. In fact, there was only one place at this horse show that she could think of that was tucked away enough that someone could sneak a horse on a trailer without worrying about someone catching them.

Emma was suddenly grateful for the way she intimately knew these horse show grounds. If her theory was right, they might still have a chance at finding Jimmie before it was too late. If they walked, or even ran, they probably wouldn't make it to the back part of the show grounds in time. If they weren't already too late, that is.

"Michael! We need to get to the truck. Now!"

Michael shot her a look of confusion but followed quickly behind Emma anyway as she sprinted full speed towards where they had parked Michael's truck. Perhaps Michael was simply used to following her headlong into trouble at this point. After they reached the truck, Emma directed Michael where to go as they headed to the far back side of the grounds.

"Slow down and park just behind those trees," Emma instructed. Michael parked the truck where Emma had instructed, and she opened the door as quietly as she could. They walked to the edge of the tree line and peered around from behind it as they stayed hidden.

There, almost hidden among several other parked trailers, was a truck running and the soft glow of trailer lights behind it. Emma held in a gasp as she saw the back end of the dark horse being loaded into the back of the trailer. The man in dark clothes shut the trailer door behind him.

"Is that Jimmie John?" Michael whispered softly in her ear.

"Definitely," she whispered back. She would know that horse's hind end anywhere. The man quickly closed the trailer doors behind the horse.

They exchanged a look that relayed they were both thinking the same thing: what did they do now? It crossed Emma's mind that even if they could somehow stop the thieves right then and there, it may not be enough to save the other horses stashed somewhere else. Also, she had no idea if they were armed.

Seconds later, truck began pulling away, and it looked like it was going to waste no time getting out of the show grounds. Michael had his phone is his hand, clearly ready to call the police. Emma and Michael stood up, hoping to catch the license plate number of the truck or trailer.

"They took the plates off!" Emma hissed under her breath. Of course they did; these guys were not stupid. Michael and Emma jogged over and ducked behind the parked truck so they wouldn't be seen as the thieves passed them.

"The police are never going to find them in time at this rate!" Emma said standing up, her voice sounding panicked.

"You want to follow them, don't you?" Michael replied, reading her mind.

"I don't really see any other option, do you?" Emma replied.

Michael paused, and Emma could see him considering her words. He tossed Emma his phone. "Call the police while I drive," Michael stated.

They quickly hopped into the truck and Michael tore down the driveway leading to the entrance of the show grounds. By the time they caught up, the trailer was just turning onto the main road. Michael hung back a little, allowing another car to get in front of them. They could still easily see the trailer from where they were on the road, but Emma guessed Michael didn't want to draw attention to themselves as they followed them.

"Smart, Michael," she thought.

Emma felt her heart hammer in her chest as they followed them down winding roads. The thieves set a blistering pace, which had Emma concerned about Jimmie John's safety in the trailer. Where were they going? They were headed straight for the coast at this point. Would they hop on the A1A and continue driving for hours? They had stolen horses from both Ocala and Wellington after all; who knew where they stashed the horses before selling them again. Emma shuddered at the other option of where the horses could be going. No way. It didn't make sense to sell horses of this caliber to anyone who wasn't paying a pretty penny for them.

Still, these horses belonged to people who loved them. God only knew what kind of people would be involved in shady sales like the ones these thieves were surely making.

They were well out of Wellington now, and as predicted, they had dead ended onto the A1A highway that ran along the ocean.

Michael's knuckles were white as he clutched the steering wheel tightly. He looked worried, sometimes shooting a concerned glance Emma's way when she was looking away. She caught him in her peripherals once or twice, wondering what he was thinking. Was he worried about her safety? At this point, Emma had faced danger more times than she would have liked and only seemed to come out of it smarter and stronger.

"I've faced scary bad guys before. I can take on a couple horse thieves," Emma thought, as if trying to convince herself of the danger that lay ahead of them was nothing. Truth be told, she couldn't imagine facing these guys without Michael at her side.

The miles passed by slowly as Michael followed behind them discreetly, always keeping a car between them and the thieves. Emma had hoped to hear police sirens by now. Did crossing the city lines throw off the police since they were so quickly in another jurisdiction? Wellington was horse country, which meant trucks and trailers were everywhere. It didn't help that the truck and trailer was about as basic looking as you could get. She was sure that was no coincidence.

Emma wondered if horse thievery was very high up on the list of what was considered an emergency. Had the 911 dispatcher downplayed it?

They had the windows rolled down, and she heard Jimmie John let out a sharp whinny once or twice. Did he sense the danger he was in? Horses had a keen sense about people; surely, he understood these people were not trustworthy. He never was one to call out while he was being hauled. Emma fought the sick feeling in her stomach knowing Jimmie John was in distress.

Should she and Michael have tried to stop the thieves before they left the horse show? Emma shook her head, clearing her mind of those thoughts. What they were doing could save not only Jimmie John, but also save the other horses taken from a terrible fate.

What felt like an eternity later, she heard Michael flip on his turn signal. Emma sat up straighter in her seat, her eyes locked back on the truck and trailer as she watched it turn off the A1A. Emma saw boats parked everywhere and several docks protruding from the coast out into the water.

Emma looked over at Michael with a quizzical expression.

"A marina?" she said, her tone giving away her confusion.

"Apparently so," Michael mumbled, his focus now on pulling into the marina without drawing any attention to themselves. Emma could see the top of the trailer above the boats, which had pulled into the area closest to the docks.

Michael drove quickly down one of the rows of boats toward where a small lot was set aside for car parking. Emma couldn't help but notice how expensive these boats looked. Most of them were massive. What kind of marina was this?

Emma knew nothing about boats, and that had her head spinning. You come to a marina to get on a boat. So how on earth were they supposed to follow them now?

The crease between Michael's eyes told her he was having similar thoughts.

"Hand me your phone," Michael instructed. Emma handed it over and Michael set it in the truck's center console. They got out of the truck and shut the doors as quietly as possible.

"We need to hurry," Michael said in a hushed tone, taking Emma's hand quickly as he began jogging toward the row of parked boats.

Michael pulled his own phone out of his pocket, dialing 911 again. He briefed the person on the other line about their location and what was going on. They were quickly approaching the front of the marina now. Michael excused himself and hung up the phone. He stopped short, hunkering down as he placed his phone under one of the parked boats on a trailer. Emma opened her mouth to ask what he was doing, but Michael grabbed her hand silently and began sprinting down the row of boats again. It was clear he had a plan, and whatever it was, they were running out of time to do it. They were too close to the workers at the marina and the thieves talking to them for Michael and Emma to have a conversation anyway.

Michael kept a quick pace, weaving around boats to stay hidden. They reached the edge of the water where Emma could see there were at least six docks that were part of this marina, all of which were full of docked boats. Michael crouched down and led her down one of the docks closest to where the trailer and truck could be seen parked in front of it. From where they were crouched, they were still hidden but had a good view of the two men talking to what appeared to be an employee of the marina. Did the marina employee know what these men were up to? Did he care? Emma felt heat creep up her neck, wishing for nothing more than to watch Michael lay out the two men who had taken Jimmie John.

The marina worker did a quick scan of the area, then nodded at one of the thieves who pulled a folded, small stack of cash from his pocket and handed it to the marina worker. The heat in Emma's neck turned into the feeling that her blood was boiling. How could someone be that shady and live with themselves? Her hands clenched into fists. She tried to calm her emotions and focus on what they were here to do: save Jimmie John.

Michael looked quickly at the men who were gathered around the back of the horse trailer now, and it was apparent they were about to unload Jimmie John. His glance shot over the boat at the end of the dock that they clearly planned to move Jimmie onto.

"Do you trust me?" Michael asked in a hushed, raspy tone. His expression was serious.

Emma nodded, eyes wide. What exactly was he about to ask her to do?

"Yes," she said, her voice coming out cracked and breathy. She could feel the tension in the air.

Michael took her hand again, giving it a quick squeeze. The look in his eyes warned her whatever was about to happen next could be dangerous. They were out of time though; the police weren't here and as soon as the boat left the marina and went Lord knows where, they may never see Jimmie John again. At that point, they would have to start the process all over again by involving the coast guard, and surely by then the thieves would be long gone. A shiver ran down her spine at the thought of just watching as they put Jimmie on that boat, never to be seen again.

Emma felt courage rise up in her. Whatever she needed to do to save Jimmie and the other horses, she was going to do it.

"It's now or never," he said. Michael's eyes were locked on hers. "Stay close and follow me." Michael's thumb brushed lightly across her cheek. "I love you, Emma," he said. Emma smiled warmly. "I love you," she whispered back.

Michael turned away and moved forward, staying crouched down enough they couldn't be seen above the boats parked on the dock. Michael stopped at the edge of the dock, turned around and put his foot on the first rail of ladder that ran from the dock to the water.

Emma swallowed hard, watching as Michael became submerged in the water, still holding on to one side of the ladder as he waited for her to climb down too. It suddenly became clear why Michael had set his phone down before they reached the docks.

Turning around, Emma climbed down the ladder until she felt the cool ocean splash against her legs. She took a deep breath, anticipating the feeling of being submerged in the water as she slid further in. Water lapped around them, but luckily the ocean was fairly quiet today. Emma held on the opposite side of the ladder facing Michael.

They looked into each other's eyes solemnly for several seconds. It was as if they were soaking in the last seconds before the really dangerous part of their mission began.

"There's going to be some sort of ladder or low point that we can use to get onto the boat," Michael whispered, swimming closer to her until he was mere inches from her. Emma nodded, and Michael continued. "We need to stay underwater as much as we can. We will be swimming close the to docks which should keep us hidden, but just in case, swim towards the boat and come up for air only when you need to and to make sure you're headed in the right direction. I'll see you at the back of the boat," Michael whispered.

"What about when we get on the boat?" Emma asked nervously, a small wave splashing her in the face lightly as she spoke. She blinked as the salt water stung her eyes.

"I'll get on first, but my guess is everyone will be in the back attempting to get Jimmie John on that boat," he said with a wink. They both knew Jimmie John could be stubborn when he didn't want to do something. Emma knew there was no way that horse was getting on this boat without a fight.

Before Emma could say anything else, she felt Michael's lips press gently against hers.

"Be careful," Michael said as he pulled away. He kissed her on the forehead and then disappeared under the dark blue water.

Emma sucked in a deep breath, then submerged herself underwater. She was suddenly glad she practically lived at her local pool all summer as a kid. Swimming lessons were something her mom had her and her siblings take for years until she was a teenager. Of course, Emma never would have guessed her strong swimming skills would be put to the test like this.

She kicked on, using every bit of her strength to push herself forward against the water's resistance. Emma felt her lungs burning and popped her head out of the water long enough to suck in a quick breath through her nose and regain her bearings. She swam on, only coming up for air when she needed to like Michael had said.

Emma was close to the boat now, but as she came up for a quick breath of air, she heard Jimmie John's shrill whinny and men yelling. Her heart sank knowing they were attempting to force him on the ship against his will. She reminded herself this was good news for her and Michael making it aboard undetected. Still, her heart hurt for the distressed horse she loved.

When Emma popped back out of the water, she was only a few feet from the back of the boat. Michael as holding onto the ladder that led to the backside of the boat. His expression softened from the worried crease it had before when he spotted her head bobbing in the water nearby. Emma swam over to Michael and the ladder, and Michael turned his attention back to the boat.

They listened for voices or movement on the boat. Emma could still hear yelling as the men struggled to get Jimmie on. Michael quickly climbed up the ladder, pausing briefly at the top so he could peek out up over the boat to see if anyone was in sight. Michael made a waving motion to Emma and pulled himself up onto the boat. Emma climbed quickly out of the water, feeling weighed down by her sopping wet clothes as she scrambled to pull herself up onto the slippery deck. Michael grabbed her hand and helped her up.

Emma's eyes ran over Michael's soaking wet body. His shirt clung to his chest, his muscles showing underneath.

"This way," Michael whispered under his breath as he led the way around the side of the boat. Emma could hear the sound of shod hooves on the boat's deck now.

"They must have finally got him on," she thought.

They stayed clung to the side of the boat that was used to store additional life vests. It was a dead end, a closed off area, besides one small section of railing facing the water, just below the enclosed staircase leading to the upper decks of the boat. Emma felt like a sitting duck as she breathed as quietly as she could, which was proving hard to do given the amount of swimming she had just done. They listened from their hiding place as the sound of horse hooves suddenly stopped. The creak and then shutting of a door followed after.

"Let's go!" a man yelled from somewhere else on the boat. Emma felt vibrations coming from below deck, followed by the rumbling of the boat's engine starting up. Emma wondered where they could possibly be taking Jimmie. Emma froze, hearing the sound of footfalls on the staircase that ran above their heads. Michael squeezed her hand reassuringly. "They can't see us here," he said under his breath. She knew that, and unless someone came over to this little storage area, they would be safe here. But still, the creaking and steps above her head had her heart racing.

They were out on the open water now, and the boat was flying across the ocean waves.

"I guess following the no wake signs goes out the window too when you're a horse thief," Emma thought, rolling her eyes at the thought.

A sharp whinny coming from somewhere inside the lower level of the ship broke her thoughts. She shot a look at Michael, hoping he understood the meaning of it.

"I'll see if I can find him once we get a little further out," Michael whispered, answering her unspoken question. Emma nodded in reply, mouthing a thank you.

Chapter Thirteen

Emma wasn't sure how long they had been on the boat now.

Thirty minutes? Forty? Maybe more.

A panicked thought had crossed her mind at one point that they would be in another country by the time the ship docked again. What then? Stranded in a foreign country without their phones or identification sounded like something straight out of a nightmare.

Michael and Emma had slumped against the side of the boat a long time ago. Her head was resting on his shoulder as she watched the wake on the side of the boat. Emma felt Michael shifting and lifted her head. Michael stood up, stretched, and then looked back down at Emma.

"I'm going to see if I can find Jimmie John," Michael whispered.

"Be careful," Emma whispered back.

It had been a long time since they had heard anyone talking or movement above them. No one had come back to the lower level of the boat. Odds were, whoever was on the boat was upstairs either resting, asleep, or driving the boat at this point.

Emma watched as Michael disappeared around the corner. Her heart raced; her palms began to feel clammy as she anxiously awaited his return.

Right about the time Emma thought she couldn't take it anymore and considered getting up to follow him, a figure emerged from around the corner. She jumped, breathing a sigh of relief once she realized it was only Michael.

"I found him," Michael whispered softly. Emma scanned his expression for any sign of how the horse was. His expression was unreadable.

"How is he?" Emma whispered back.

"Follow me," Michael said, helping her up.

Emma followed closely behind Michael, her hand in his as they tip-toed quietly across the boat. They were near the middle of the ship now, and Michael paused at a large, sliding door. He tossed Emma a worried look but opened the door slowly without saying anything else.

Emma gasped audibly at the sight.

She had wondered when she first saw the yacht-like boat where on earth they planned to store a horse. Now, she understood.

At one point this must have been some sort of room with an open sitting area. They had converted it, taking out everything in the room and laying down rubber mats. There was no bedding, and the room was hot and humid. Only one window was barely cracked open. Jimmie was tied tightly to a metal ring that had been installed on the wall. No hay or water was in sight.

Jimmie John let out a low, friendly nicker at the site of his human friend. Emma's heart broke. She walked over to the horse, running her hand across his dark, sweaty coat.

"We will get you out of here soon, bud," Emma said, tears welling in her eyes and then spilling across her cheeks. She cradled the gelding's head in her hands.

Emma suddenly felt off balance. The boat was downshifting and slowing down.

"We need to go!" Michael's hushed voice said behind her.

Emma planted a quick kiss on his velvety nose before sliding out of the door behind Michael. He slid it shut, and they power-walked silently back to their hiding place.

A very small island was becoming visible now. The boat was approaching a wide, wooden dock stretched across the water from the beach. Emma wondered where they were. The island looked so small though; it wouldn't surprise her if it was one of those private islands someone owned. She shuddered to think how many horses they would have had to steal and sell to purchase their own island.

Emma and Michael stayed hidden as the boat finished docking. Jimmie began whinnying loudly once the boat stopped moving, clearly wondering where he had been taken. Emma's heart broke for him, and she told herself it would only be a matter of time before she rescued him.

Although in this very moment, she wasn't sure how they were going to pull that off. They had no cell phones, not that they would have reception way out here in the middle of the ocean anyway, and it was at least three men against the two of them. Emma had never expected their relationship to be put to the test quite like this. But here they were, and all they had was each other to make sure they, and the horses, made it out of here alive. She wondered if the police were looking for them way out here. When the police arrived at the marina after Michael called them, surely that marina worker would have played dumb since he was getting paid off.

Emma heard the sound of horse hooves on the boat deck followed by the soft thudding sound of hooves on the wooden dock. Emma fought the urge to chase after Jimmie John. Michael's hand reached across her lap, his hand resting gently on her knee. He must have guessed how she was feeling. Emma realized that if any two people could pull this off, it was her and Michael. After all, this wasn't their first run in with bad guys.

They sat there in silence listening intently to the sound of the men on the boat. The two men that had taken Jimmie from the show grounds were already off the boat, and the man who had been the boats captain it was finally walking down the wooden dock as well.

Emma blew out a breath she didn't know she was holding.

"What now?" Emma said to Michael, still at a whisper. No one was in ear shot now, but for some reason she still felt the need to speak in a hushed tone.

"Now, we get off this boat and find those horses," Michael stated. The determination on his face comforted Emma a little. It was clear he was determined to find the horses just as much as she was. The other horses had to be here. At least some of them. She just hoped they weren't too late.

Michael stood up, looking around the boat. He grabbed rope and a bag used to hold extra life vests, emptying it out. He searched the boat, adding a few other items to the bag. Once again, Emma was grateful for Michael's background. Between his years as a boy scout and working for his grandfather at his cattle ranch, he would be prepared for what they were about to face.

Emma felt a little useless, wondering how she could be helpful. Maybe once they found the horses, she could be of use then.

Michael headed towards the front of the boat. He peeked out from behind one of the ships walls, scanning the dock and beach area thoroughly.

"Ready?" Michael asked, turning to face Emma. His arm slid around her waist; his eyes locked onto hers. Emma was sure in that moment she had never trusted anyone as much as she trusted Michael right then.

"Ready," Emma stated.

Michael took Emma's hand as they climbed off the boat and onto the dock. They picked up a quick jog; no need wasting time out in the open where they could easily be seen. Luckily, the sun was setting, and it was getting darker. A sandy path became visible when they reached the beach. They slipped into the tropical forest area parallel to the path so they could follow it and still stay hidden.

Emma looked around the at the lush vegetation and palm trees that seemed to go on for miles. This island was stunning. Too bad it was being used for horse theft. She couldn't help but think about how this was the kind of place she could see herself honeymooning in as they weaved through the forest.

The faint sound of male voices talking in the distance could be heard now. Michael led Emma even further from the path just to be safe. They crouched down, peering from the foliage from a safe distance.

Emma saw the two men who had taken Jimmie John talking to another man, presumably the boat's captain, in front of a run-down looking pole barn. The roof was rusted, but the outside of the metal barn looked newer. It had one large sliding door on the front of it, facing their direction.

"...tomorrow," one of the men said. They had apparently caught them at the end of a conversation.

"Have all five on the dock by 7:00 am," said the captain of the boat.

One of the men made a grunting sound but said nothing else. He turned and headed the other direction, towards another path, this one much narrower, that led towards the far-right side of the island. The two other men followed behind him towards the narrow path.

Emma noticed just how dark it was now. Michael and Emma stayed hidden in the forest another few minutes just to be safe, listening for any sign that the men planned to come back. Emma hoped wherever that path led, it was far enough from here that they couldn't hear what they were about to do.

"I think they are gone for the night," Michael said in a low voice. He stood up and walked to the edge of the forest, into the clearing towards the pole barn. Emma followed closely behind him.

Michael slowly opened the sliding door of the pole barn, being careful not make much noise. They slipped through the small opening he made, quickly sliding it shut behind them.

The smell of horse feces and urine was overpowering the moment they shut the door. Emma coughed, her eyes watering, holding her shirt up to her nose as she fought nausea.

It was pitch black. Emma couldn't even see her hand extended in front of her. She heard Michael unzip the bag he had taken from the boat and heard a clicking sound. Suddenly the pole barn was illuminated by the flashlight he had turned on.

Emma gasped, probably louder than she should have. She felt dizzy, her hand reflexively reached for Michael's for balance. Five horses were huddled in the corner of the pole barn. Some looked like had been here awhile and were covered in filth.

"Jimmie," Emma breathed, spotting him amongst the other horses. One other horse looked fairly clean, like Jimmie. Emma assumed this horse had recently been stolen too. The blaze on one of the other horses caught her attention.

"I know that horse!" Emma said quietly, pointing at the chestnut standing near the front of the pack.

"Is he one of the horses stolen from Ocala?" Michael asked, his eyes running over each horse, a crease forming between his eyes.

"Yes! That's the horse Lily and I were looking for at the Ocala horse show. The owner showed us a picture of him. That's definitely the same horse," Emma said, recalling the day she had first discovered horses were being stolen. Here they were in front of her, on some secluded island. Her heart swelled knowing she had found them.

"You haven't rescued them yet," she reminded herself.

Emma walked over to the horses, running her hand across the neck of a chestnut. He nuzzled her arm with his nose.

"We will get you guys out of here, I promise," Emma whispered.

Jimmie walked over to Emma, and she rested her forehead on the bridge of his nose. This was no place any horse should ever have to be, even for a short while.

"Em, we should probably get out of here, just in case someone comes back to check on the horses," Michael said softly.

"Ok," Emma murmured, taking a few extra seconds to say goodbye to Jimmie John.

Emma walked reluctantly behind Michael. He shut off the flashlight before sliding open the door just enough for them to slip out. He peered around the corner, making sure no one was outside before they walked out of the barn.

Michael and Emma scurried back to the safety of the tropical forest. Michael laced his fingers through Emma's and they stayed close to the sandy path that led back to the beach. It was so dark now that once they were a little way from the pole barn, they walked directly down the path itself. It was far too challenging clambering through thick brush in the dark than it had been in the daylight.

The full moon cast shadows behind them as they walked down the beach, the opposite direction of where the men had headed, presumably towards where they were sleeping.

"I figured we should get a little distance so we won't be seen in case anyone comes out to the beach early tomorrow morning," Michael said.

Emma nodded. "Are we sleeping on the beach?"

"It's probably the most comfortable place to sleep, and the beach curves around, so we should be safe here," Michael stated. He stopped in a place that had a little inlet where there was still sand and trees blocked them from view. Still, they were so far down from the dock now that they wouldn't be visible regardless.

Michael sat in the sand and Emma sat beside him. He pulled two water bottles and some snacks from the bag they took from the boat. Michael looked like he was turning over a plan in his mind, so Emma waited for him to speak.

"I was hoping the marine radio was still on the boat, but when I was looking for supplies before, I noticed it was missing. That was my original plan, call for help once we got to shore. I bet they took it with them," Michael said. Emma wondered if maybe the captain didn't trust the two men who picked up Jimmie. She sensed there was some tension during their conversation.

"That's probably our best shot at getting ahold of the coast guard." Emma said, stating the obvious.

"It's our *only* chance. There's no way anyone has cell service out here. One way or another, we need to get our hands on one of those boat radios. I have a feeling a different boat is coming to pick the horses up tomorrow, just based on what I heard those men saying. Plus, there is no way five horses fit in that room Jimmie was in. We need to get on that new boat and get on the radio," Michael said.

"How on earth are we going to do that?" Emma said, looking concerned.

"Well, if you're up for it, we need a distraction." Michael said, shooting her a concerned look.

Emma lifted an eyebrow curiously.

"Here's what I'm thinking. We obviously need to wait for the new boat to arrive first. Once it does, I don't think we will have a lot of time between when it arrives and when the horses are loaded on the boat. That's where you come in. If the horses get loose at just the right time, the men will be scrambling to catch them. I don't want you getting hurt, and since those guys will be onto to you the moment they get loose, the best thing I could think of is to get on Jimmie John bareback and get far away from them. Meanwhile, I'll sneak on the boat while everyone is distracted trying to round up the horses. There should hopefully only be one person, the new ship's captain, on the boat at that point. I'm guessing they don't want more people to know what's going on here than absolutely necessary, and those two men who took Jimmie are the ones loading the horses up. I should be able to use the element of surprise to take him out and get to the radio to call a distress signal. Then, we just have to hope the coast guard comes in hot," Michael said shrugging, like he hadn't just come up with what Emma considered the best possible plan.

"Michael Hale, you are a genius. I knew I loved you for a reason," Emma teased.

Michael smiled at Emma and leaned back, resting his head against the powder white sand. Emma rested her head on Michael's chest. His heartbeat was the only thing she could hear above the waves crashing against the shore.

It had been a long day and suddenly Emma felt overwhelmed with exhaustion. Michael seemed to be feeling the same way.

"My body clock will wake me up well before 7:00 am, don't worry," Michael said, wrapping his arms around Emma. Once again, he had read her mind.

It wasn't long before her eyes felt so heavy she couldn't keep them open.

Despite the danger tomorrow promised, she felt perfectly safe in that moment wrapped in Michael's arms with the ocean sounds singing her to sleep.

ell

"Em."

Was this a dream? Emma felt herself stuck between reality and the dream she was trapped in.

"Emma!" Michael's voice was clear now, yanking her from sleep.

"I'm...I'm awake," she said groggily. Emma pushed herself halfway up, leaning against her elbows as she blinked, taking in her surroundings. That's right, she was on an island.

"Em, the boat, it's getting ready to dock," Michael said.

Emma looked out across the water, and saw what Michael was referring to; a large boat approaching the dock. She could hear the rumbling of the boat's engine in the distance.

"It's not 7:00 am yet, is it?" Emma said, looking up at the sky. The sun had barely risen. It had to be just after 6:00 am, based on when the sun rose this time of year.

"Could just be getting here early," Michael replied, shrugging.

Emma stood up, dusting sand off her back and legs. It was now or never if they wanted to save the horses and themselves.

"Let's head back up the beach. When we get close enough that we could be spotted, we will cut through the forest. Do you think you could find your way through the forest yourself back to the pole barn?"

Emma nodded. "I can do that," she said, sounding a little braver than she felt.

"Good. I need to wait close to the beach so that the moment you signal me the horses are loose, I will make my move. Got it?"

"Got it," Emma agreed. Nerves fluttered in her gut. She reminded herself she had the easy job. Wait for the right moment, sneak into the barn, get on Jimmie John and let the other horses loose. It sounded simple enough in her head. She trusted Jimmie John with her life. Which was a good thing considering that's exactly what was at stake.

They headed down the beach the way they came last night. Emma felt much more exposed this time in the daylight. They cut back into the forest just before the beach curved around, which was what had kept them hidden until now.

Emma pushed aside lush plants as they made their way as quietly as possible through the forest. They could see where the forest gave way to a clear area, where the path leading to the pole barn was located. Michael paused, turning around. This was it; this is where she was on her own.

"You can do this, Em. You are the bravest, smartest woman I have ever met," Michael whispered, his hands gently cradling the back of her neck. Emma suddenly felt more nervous for Michael. He would be directly facing one, or more, of the bad guys, after all.

"Promise me you will be careful," Emma whispered back, getting lost in his gorgeous, green eyes. Somehow, he never looked more attractive than he did right now. Perhaps the life-or-death situation had something to with it.

"I promise," he said, inches from her face now. He leaned in a little closer, his lips lightly brushed across hers, moving slowly. Emma pulled him in closer, her body pressed against his. The kiss intensified. If something happened to either of them,

Emma wanted to make sure Michael knew exactly how she felt. A memorable kiss seemed to be the best way to do just that.

Emma pulled away, feeling lightheaded. She took in a long, slow breath, letting herself come back to reality. They held one another's gaze a couple more seconds before she turned away from him and she headed in the direction of a pole barn.

"Hey Em? Give those boys a run for their money," he said with a wink.

A devious look crossed her face. "I'll be on Jimmie John, remember? They won't know what hit them," Emma said, smirking before she turned back around.

Emma felt the fear and nerves turn into anger. An anger fueled by the mistreatment of a horse she loved like her own. Michael's words rang in her ears. These men had messed with the wrong girl and the wrong horse; they just didn't know it yet.

Emma crouched down in the same place they had watched the men talking near the barn last night. The coast was clear in front of the barn so far. Luckily, it was still much earlier than the captain had instructed the other men to get the horses loaded onto the boat.

"Good, they must still be wherever they were sleeping," she thought.

Emma closed her eyes, listening for the sound of voices. In the distance, the same direction they had gone when they left for the night last night, she could hear men laughing and talking. They sounded a safe distance away.

"It's now or never," she thought. If they were outside and just down the path, they could head this was at any time.

Emma jogged into the clearing, opening the door and slipping through. She shut the door most of the way, leaving just enough of a crack she could easily slide the door back open from Jimmie John's back.

Several lead ropes were lumped together in a pile near the doors entrance. Emma sifted through them, finding the longest one.

Walking over to the horses, whose ears were all pricked in her direction curiously now, she spotted Jimmie John close to the far right corner.

"Hey, bud. It's just me," Emma murmured. "We are going to get you and your friends out of here. You just have to trust me."

Emma clipped one side of the lead rope to his halter, tying a tight knot on the other to create makeshift reins. Emma had never ridden Jimmie bareback, but his wide, Warmblood figure was perfect for bareback riding. She thanked her lucky stars for all the bonding time the two of them had in the past. Emma was going to be relying on that mutual trust to get them through this.

Emma turned her head reflexively as the sound of male voices conversing could be heard easily now.

"They must be getting close!" she thought, her heart racing now.

Time was up.

Emma flipped the makeshift reins over Jimmie's head. Emma used all her strength to push herself off the ground, grabbing mane to help pull her the rest of the way onto the tall gelding's back. Jimmie took a half sidestep in surprise, his ears swiveling back.

"It's just me, Jimmie," Emma murmured as she stroked his neck. He stood still now at the sound of her familiar voice.

One of the men laughed loudly. They had to be merely feet away from the pole barn now.

"So much for my plan," she thought.

Emma had hoped to have the upper hand, let the horses out at the moment she heard them exactly where they were now, far enough away to give her and the other horses a head start.

Emma gently squeezed Jimmie forward, getting a little closer to the door. If she opened the door herself now, they would probably be right in front of her. Being off balance in the position she needed to be in to slide the door open from

Jimmie's back would not be doing her any favors. Her only option now was to come blasting out of door at a full force gallop the moment they opened the door and hope for the best. Horses, being the herd animals they were, would hopefully follow Jimmie's lead and come barreling out behind her. They still held the element of surprise, which would be in her favor.

Emma felt her heart hammer in her chest. Her breathing was shallow, her hands turning white as she held her makeshift reins in a death grip. Jimmie danced under her; he sensed her nerves. Emma remembered the way Jimmie launched off his hind legs the moment the buzzer sounded in the jumper ring. She may not have a buzzer, but maybe a whistle would be enough to get him going in the same way.

Emma heard the one man reprimand the other for leaving the barn door ajar. They were right in front of the door now. Emma stared the crack in the door down, as it began to slowly slide open. She waited for the moment it was just wide enough.

"GO!" she thought.

The man who had opened the door stood frozen and wide-eyed. His jaw dropped the moment the door was open enough to allow light for him to see the young woman sitting bareback on the almost black horse.

Emma felt a smirk tug at her lips at his expression. A sharp whistle escaped her lips a split second later, and she wrapped her legs around the horse. Jimmie launched forward with everything in him. The gelding charged down the now open door, almost plowing over the man who still stood in the doorway, jaw dropped. He dove out of the way just in time to not get trampled by Jimmie and the small herd of horses that were now galloping behind him out of the pole barn.

"GET THEM!" one of the men yelled behind her.

The smirk was still spread across her face, growing wider with each stride.

"Now!" Emma yelled as loud as she could, hoping Michael could hear her.

Emma and Jimmie galloped down the path towards the beach. Wind coming off the ocean whirled past her ears, thudding hooves on the sandy ground was the only other thing she could hear now. Emma was relieved when she saw Michael was sprinting towards the boat as they came off the path, galloping out onto the open beach.

Emma sat back, turning Jimmie in the direction where she and Michael spent the night. Emma glanced behind her, and saw Michael still running full speed, on the dock now.

"*He's going to make it!*" she thought. The other men still hadn't emerged onto the beach. There was no way they would see Michael at this rate; he would be safely on the boat by the time they got to the beach and chasing her the opposite direction.

Emma looked to her left where two of the other horses were almost keeping pace with Jimmie. They tossed their heads, and one of them crow hopped. Emma smiled widely; these horses were finally free of their captors, and they knew it. Looking under her arm, she saw the other three were galloping right on Jimmie's heels.

Emma made a kissing sound to Jimmie, opening his stride up even more. He reveled in his own power, kicking up sand behind him as he pushed forward. Emma shut her eyes a moment, soaking in the feeling of flying across the sand. It was like a weight was lifting. Michael was going to call for help. The horses were safe.

And no one could possibly catch them now.

Emma wasn't sure how long they had been hiding out in a small clearing just behind a little wall of palm trees and brush.

They were on the far side of the island now. She sat on Jimmie's back still, allowing him to lip at the vegetation around them. From her vantage point, she could hear and see anyone coming and take off again if need be. The other horses had followed behind them the whole way and were now lipping hungrily at the vegetation around them too. She was pretty sure they hadn't been fed properly, so these horses were happy to stand here as long as they had something to eat. And with a whole forest of plant-life around them, there was no running out of that anytime soon.

Emma heard a fast, rumbling sound. Another boat.

She nudged Jimmie forward to get a better view of the coast further down. Her eyes scanned to water frantically.

Nothing.

Emma felt her heart rate pick up and her mouth go dry. What if things had gone wrong with Michael when he was trying to overtake the captain? What if the boat was circling the island looking for them?

She held her breath, listening to the sound of a boat far away grow louder. They were circling back and heading her way again. Emma swallowed hard, leaning forward as she strained to see as far down the coast as she could. The sun reflected off the water, making it hard to see. Both hands gripped the makeshift reins, ready to run any second. She ran through all of her options in her mind. Go further into the brush to the other side of the island or back on the beach where they were easily seen but could go much faster?

Emma could see it was a smaller boat now. She squinted, trying to make out any of the details on it. It was white, with red around the bottom of it. Words were painted on the side. It was getting closer now, but what did it say?

"Coast guard!" she said, half gasping as she spoke.

Emma clucked to Jimmie who trotted out of the forest onto the powder-white beach sand. Emma raised her hand above her head, waving frantically at the boat. It turned in her direction moments later, speeding across the water. She saw someone waving from the back of the coast guard boat.

They were close to shore now and slowed to a stop. Someone in the boat dove into the water and swam her way. He popped his head out of the water moments later and stood up in the shallow water, drenched head to toe.

"Michael!" Emma yelled, able to recognize him now. She thought her heart might stop. Relief flooded her. He was safe. They were all safe now. Emma slid from Jimmie's back, one hand still on the lead rope, running as fast as she could with Jimmie jogging behind her.

Emma wrapped her arms around Michael's soaking wet body the moment he was within her reach. His arms twisted firmly around her waist, pulling her in tight. They stood there a long time, wrapped up in each other's arms. Emma's fingers twisted through Michael's wet hair, and her lips met his. Both hands were on her cheeks now, his lips pressing firmly against hers.

He pulled away, a glimmer in his green eyes that hinted there was something he was excited about.

Suddenly, he dropped to one knee right there on the sand, both his hands clasping one of hers between them. Was he really about to do what she thought he was going to?

"Emma Walker, I love you. I never thought I would love anyone the way I love you. You are my best friend. The last twenty-four hours confirmed something I have been thinking about lately anyway. I know it may seem soon, but Emma, will you marry me?"

Michael's green eyes were lit up like the fourth of July.

Emma waited for the panic she felt when Liam had proposed to surface. That feeling that she was making a decision that would affect the rest of her life that had her running for the hills last time. The thoughts that screamed she was too young, that this was too fast. Emma paused, barely breathing, waiting. But this time, not one single thought bubbled up telling her to run or consider what a monumental decision this was. There was only one thought flashing across her mind.

"Yes!" Emma said, her voice breaking with emotion halfway through the word.

Michael wrapped both arms around her, sweeping her off her feet and spinning her around before his lips met hers again.

It had always been Michael. Emma never quite believed in soulmates until she met him.

And Michael was hers. She knew that now.

"To Emma and Michael!" Lily said, holding her champagne glass up. Cathy, Clara, and Sam raised their glasses up as well. Mandy, who was on a video call on Emma's laptop, raised her glass up as well from across the country.

"Thanks Lily. And thank you everyone for coming out to this last minute dinner. Michael and I just wanted to tell the people closest to us about our engagement in person, and we figured we may as well make a night of it," Emma said, beaming.

"We have a lot to celebrate today. As of this morning, we were told all the stolen horses have been officially reunited with their owners," Michael said proudly.

Champagne glasses clinked together as everyone at the patio table just outside Emma's house at Live Oak's Farm said "cheers" in unison. Each of them took a sip of champagne before setting their glasses back down.

"What's the update on the investigation of the horse thieves?" Clara asked Emma.

"Apparently the horse thieves involved in this operation have been stealing and selling horses for almost a year now. The detective I spoke to this morning said there were maybe about ten people total involved in the stealing and shipping of the horses to the private island. They discovered the island is owned by some guy named Joey Langsmith whose father was incredibly wealthy, and Joey inherited the island from his father. Joey then gambled his entire trust fund away and was left with nothing but the piece of land in the middle of the ocean. So apparently he then met some guy at a casino who he owed money to, who says he's running a small horse thieving business and asks Joey if he wants to provide them access to the island in exchange for a cut of the profits. Joey agreed to the deal because he had next to no money at this point, and that's how the operation grew from there.

They started stealing horses in other parts of Florida, but probably realized the horses worth the most are conveniently located together in Ocala and Wellington, which is why we just started noticing a pattern once they started stealing horses from the shows. They were shipping the horses on boats from the island to other small countries in the Caribbean to be sold on horse trading black market. They said Michael and I took down what was becoming one of the biggest horse thief operations on the east coast. They said they are currently searching for the horses stolen prior to the ones we found that have been reported missing in other parts of Florida, but they would have never had a chance at finding any of them if Michael and I hadn't found the island," Emma said, smiling over at Michael and taking his hand.

Emma felt good about the five horses they had reunited with their owners and knowing there were many more out there that had a good chance at being found thanks to their bravery.

Lily shook her head in disbelief. "Leave it to the two of you to get engaged while busting a massive horse thief operation."

Everyone at the table laughed. Honestly, it seemed fairly appropriate, given how often danger seemed to follow them.

Emma almost couldn't believe how lucky she was as she looked around the table.

She now had everything she could have ever dreamed of; and then some.

Epilogue

"Emma, if you cry, you *will* ruin your makeup," Mandy scolded her.

Makeup that Mandy had spent several hours putting on her.

Emma took in a long, slow breath, trying to control her emotions. But how could she?

Valentine stood in front of her, led over to the back side of her house by Lily. Valentine was the cleanest Emma had ever seen her horse with white flowers tucked into her mane and tail. The mare looked at her, ears pricked, staring at the large, white, funny looking dress her owner was in. To be fair, it was a far cry from the dirty breeches and t-shirt Emma was normally in.

"Maybe the ballgown style dress was a little much," Emma said, blushing. After all, this was an outdoor wedding.

"Nonsense!" Cathy exclaimed, smoothing the front of Emma's wedding dress. Cathy had insisted on buying Emma's wedding dress, of course. It made sense *she* would think it was not too much. Still, Emma couldn't help but feel like she was Disney princess in this dress. Perhaps it wasn't too much after all.

"Don't worry Cathy, there won't be a particle of dust on this horse that will transfer to Emma's dress," Lily said, clearly proud of her grooming skills.

"Honey, you look perfect," Chrissy, Emma's mother, said. She was dabbing tears from the corner of her eyes, and it was far from the first time she had cried that day.

"It's time!" Clara said, peeking her head around the corner of the house.

Emma felt butterflies doing somersaults in her stomach. It was the type of day you wonder about for most of your young adult life. Emma gathered her dress in her hands and walked over to Valentine. Lily pulled the mounting block over and Emma swung her leg over the mare's bare back. Cathy began spreading the dress over Valentine's back until it was draped perfectly.

"We will see you at the altar," Mandy said with a wink as she, Clara, Cathy, and Lily headed away from the house towards the alter at the far end of Live Oaks Farm.

It had been Emma's idea to have the wedding here, surrounded by the people and horses that meant so much to her. Cathy had not been thrilled about not being able to throw her the massive grand ballroom style wedding she had originally suggested, but Emma had a feeling Cathy would still be outdoing herself today. It was one of the many reasons she was so glad Cathy was still like family to her, despite the fact she hadn't decided to marry Liam.

Emma waited for about five minutes, as she had been instructed, before asking Valentine to walk forward. Her hand ran across her mare's velvety soft coat, and she was suddenly glad to have her horse by her side for a day as important as today.

Emma and Valentine walked on, and she felt the butterflies get more intense the closer they got. Finally, she reached a point where the rolling hills gave way, and she could see the rows of chairs set up leading to the well-decorated alter.

Her heart stopped for half a beat as her eyes connected with Michael's. Suddenly, the butterflies and anxiety melted away. Emma smiled widely as she and Valentine made their way down the aisle. She saw so many familiar faces from back home as well as new friends she had made since arriving in Florida.

They were at the end of the aisle now. Emma stared at Michael and the look on his face; she was sure it was a look she would remember for the rest of her life. Lily stepped forward, taking a hold of Valentine's reins as Emma carefully slid off her mare's back and adjusted her dress when both feet were on the ground. Lily led Valentine back over to where the other bridesmaids stood.

Michael stepped forward, taking her hand in his as they approached the officiant. They stood face to face, eyes locked.

"I love you," Michael whispered so only she could hear, his lips inches from hers.

"I love you too," Emma whispered back.

The sun painted a pink-orange sky behind them, and the light breeze blew the Spanish moss hanging from a large oak tree directly behind them.

"Let's hear it for the bride and groom!" the DJ announced as Emma and Michael made their way to the dance floor.

Emma had been right, of course. Cathy had outdone herself. A large event tent was heavily decorated with twinkle lights that were strung up throughout. Emma had been blown away by just how stunning everything had turned out. Even for Cathy's standards, this was impressive.

The slow country love song began playing and Michael took her right hand in his, an arm wrapped around the hollow of her back.

"Have I told you how stunning you look in that dress?" Michael asked, spinning her around the dance floor.

"Only a few times," she teased. Still, a warm smile spread across her lips. Cameras flashed and Michael dipped Emma mid-step.

"Where did you learn to do *that*?" Emma asked, wide-eyed.

"Cathy," he murmured, a smirk tugging at his lips.

"Of course," she thought.

Michael's lips pressed lightly on her neck, and a soft groan escaped her. He pulled her back up, landing Emma on her feet lightly.

"Just think, this time tomorrow we will be back on a private island, only this time, there won't be any bad guys or stolen horses," Michael said with a wink.

Emma shook her head, thinking about Cathy's generous gift of renting a private island home for them for their honeymoon. As if she hadn't done enough for them already.

"Private island, you, and no bad guys? Count me in," Emma said, smiling.

Michael twirled Emma around, her dress flowing out around her, then brought her close to him again.

Emma rested her chin on Michael's shoulder, her eyes scanning the tent full of her loved ones smiling at them.

Emma was quite sure this was the best day of her life.

The End

The "Impelled" Series continues with book four – featuring / telling the stories of side characters from the series Lily and Sam, titled "Running Out" is now available on Amazon!

Also, a prequel featuring teenaged Emma Walker, set years before book one begins, titled "When You're Young" is also available on Amazon!

Be sure to subscribe to my newsletter on my website, sarahwelkbaynumauthor.com, and follow my author page on Amazon for updates on new releases!

Notes from the Author

Thank you to the readers who took a chance and read my debut novel. I hope you enjoyed reading it as much as I loved writing it!

If you enjoyed it, please be sure to leave a review so others have a chance to find it as well.

Reviews help me tremendously as an independently published author and it also helps other readers!

Sincerely,

Sarah Welk Baynum

Subscribe to my newsletter (sign up form on my website home page) to be the first to know about the release date for the next book in the _Impelled_ series!

https://sarahwelkbaynumauthor.com/

About the Author

Sarah Welk Baynum has an extensive equestrian background which became the inspiration behind her debut novel "Impelled."

While writing her novels, Sarah draws from previous experience as a working student, show groom, barn manager, working for FarmVet and other various jobs in the horse industry over the years both in her hometown and in Wellington &

Ocala, Florida. Sarah also attended Otterbein University and majored in Equine Business and Facility Management.

Sarah still owns horses and actively competes in show jumping and three-day eventing, and horses have been a big part of her life since the age of twelve. Her first horse may have been a gelding, but she has a bias for mares and has primarily owned mares throughout the years.

Besides writing equestrian novels, Sarah also writes articles for Sidelines Magazine.

When she isn't writing or riding, Sarah also enjoys competing in local and national singing competitions, and mainly sings country music.

Today, Sarah lives in her hometown just outside of Columbus, Ohio, with her family which includes her husband, her two dogs, two cats and her two mares Tilly (a warmblood) and Letty (an off the track thoroughbred).

Made in United States
Orlando, FL
30 November 2024

54625124R00114